CAMDEN

A FOUR SONS STORY

Mandy,

XOXO

[signature]

K WEBSTER

Mandy,

xoxo

Camden
Copyright © 2018 K Webster

Cover Design: All By Design
Photo: Adobe Stock
Editor: Word Nerd Editing
Formatting: Raven Designs

I am intelligent, unassuming,
and the son of two murdered parents.
I'm calculating, damaged, and seek revenge.

I'll do whatever it takes to further my agenda, even if it
means seducing my way into a bed I don't belong.
Anything to make the ones who've hurt me pay.

My name is Camden Pearson.

I am focused, fierce, and power-hungry.
The youngest of four brothers.
People assume I'm the baby, but I grew up a long time
ago.

*** *This series should be read in order to understand the plot.* ***

DEDICATION

To my husband—I love you.

WARNING

The hero in this book is a Pearson.

———— PROLOGUE

Tick. Tick. Tick.

I watch the big hand on my watch move along with the beats of my heart.

My big brother scared him away last year.

But not for good.

He came back.

Today marks three times this summer.

Don't look at him. Don't think about him.

Tick. Tick. Tick.

"Such a good boy," he rumbles, making me shiver all over.

I will not cry. Dad doesn't like it when we cry if we fall or get hurt. *"Be a man,"* Dad always says. *"Pearsons are tough."* I don't feel so tough.

My eyes remain glued to my watch—the same watch my grandad, Roy, gave me on my birthday this year.

Tick. Tick. Tick.

I wish I were with Grandad in New York. I wish I were playing in the pool with my brothers. I wish I were helping Dad marinade the steaks.

Anywhere but here.

"Shhh, don't tell your father. It's our secret."

My eyes remain tear free and I don't look at *him*. I never do. All I offer is a clipped nod of my head, hoping he'll go away soon.

Tick. Tick. Tick.

He rights his clothes, then slips from my room. The moment he's gone, I let out a heavy breath of relief. Tears well in my eyes, but I quickly blink them back.

Tick. Tick. Tick.

I scrub off the mess he left on my stomach with my discarded shirt. I toss the shirt at my hamper when the door creaks back open. Terror overwhelms me, and this time, I can't hold in my tears. The moment I see my father's friend Mateo, I let out a choked sob before I can stop myself.

"Your dad was looking for—" He stalks toward me. I don't flinch from Mateo. Mateo is like an uncle to me. A *good* uncle. "What's wrong?"

"I-I-I..." I trail off, imploring him to reach inside my head. To pluck out what I'm too embarrassed to say.

"Bad dream?" he asks. "Eric said you were up here

napping."

Tears streak down my cheeks, and I hastily swipe them away. My room reeks with *his* scent. How can Mateo not smell the evil still clinging to every surface?

"Yep," I tell him, my voice hardening. "Bad dream."

My tears dry, and I meet Mateo's confused stare with an emotionless one of my own.

"Anything I can do to help?" he asks softly, ruffling the hair on top of my head. Mateo is everything in a father my dad isn't. I've seen how he adores his wife and daughter. Unlike my father. Just once, I wish my dad would ruffle my hair and tell me he loves me. Just once, I wish he'd charge into my room at the exact moment the monster from my dreams come to life is here. Just once, I'd love to see him rip him to shreds.

Just once.

"Camden," Mateo tries again, his dark brows furrowed in concern. "I can help. Whatever it is, just tell me."

Not this. I can't tell him this.

What if he doesn't believe me? I know Dad wouldn't. The only person who would believe me is Nixon, and now that it's happened three times, I'm not sure I want Nixon to know.

"Can you help me put a lock on my door? I have money saved that Grandad sent me."

His features darken. "Is someone hurting you?"

I lift my chin and smile. My smiles have always gotten me out of trouble. Teachers, my friends' parents, adults in general. Well, aside from one adult, and he doesn't deserve my smiles. "Nope. I just want a lock. I'll be a teenager soon, and teenagers need privacy." I always hear my older brothers Hayden and Brock beating off in their rooms. Teenagers definitely need privacy.

Mateo's face breaks into a grin—the same grin he regards his daughter Elma with. "Boy, you're barely ten. Don't rush growing up."

Too late for that, Uncle Teo.

"I need one that'll keep the monsters out," I tell him, my bottom lip trembling despite my not wanting it to.

He doesn't understand the monsters are real. That they don't come from under beds or in closets, they come straight through my bedroom door. Sneaky and quick. While no one is watching.

"Come on," he says after a long pause. "The party is getting wild out back. I'll run you to the hardware store and we'll grab the stuff we need. They'll never miss us."

I smile again.

After today, the monster won't get back into my room. I won't have to tell Mateo or my dad or one of my older brothers. I won't have to tell anyone.

It's our secret.

This time, I don't shudder at those words.

It's our secret—one I'll take to my grave.

ONE ——————

C A M D E N

EIGHT YEARS LATER...

THEY SAY THE PAST MAKES A PERSON. DEFINES who they are. Molds and shapes them into who they'll become.

I say fuck the past.

The past is dead to me.

Just like both my parents.

I feel like every passing moment is a drop in the bucket that will fill and overflow one day. That bucket is your wealth. The goddamn future. I want mine so full, it drowns out everyone around me.

Until then, I drop, drop, drop.

"Camden!" Mateo booms from his office.

I step into the room and regard the man—the very man I always assumed was perfect in every way compared to my father. Now, I realize every man has secrets. Even Mateo. Mateo Bonilla is a dirty old man.

Not like some dirty men I know, just your typical old guy hooking up with younger women to make himself feel better. He married once for love, but his first wife died from cancer. Next time he ties the knot will be purely for his ego.

His fiancée is twenty years his junior.

And my old babysitter.

I stifle a snort and regard my father's longtime friend with a wide grin. "Uncle Teo."

He stands and rounds his massive desk to pull me in for a hug. For a moment, I relax and take it for what it is. Mateo, despite who he's going to marry, is still good. He would never hurt me. I wish I could say the same.

Sometimes, those drops in the bucket splash onto others like acid. Collateral damage. I have a slight pang in my chest, but after years of learning how to control my emotions out of necessity, I push away the weak moment.

Some things are necessary.

Hurting Mateo is necessary.

"How's college treating you, kiddo?" he asks as he pulls away and tugs at my necktie.

I chuckle and step away from him, already over the nearness to another man and needing some breathing room. "Easy," I say, shrugging. "How's working for my big brother?"

He rolls his eyes and nods his head to the right where Hayden's office is. "We don't work for him, punk. We work *with* him. You know that. And for the record, Trevor and Hayden still butt heads."

No surprise there.

The evidence suggested Trevor didn't sleep with our mom and conceive my brother Nixon, but not everyone believed the evidence. Especially not my oldest brother, Hayden. At one point, I swear, he was prepared take that piece of the past to his grave and then obsess over it well into eternity.

I, on the other hand, don't care.

Nixon is my brother, and that's all that matters to me. Our mother was a cheating whore. End of story.

"I'll talk to him." I tilt my head to the side and lift my brow slightly. My talks come with a price. Everyone knows this. Question is, are they willing to pay it?

He huffs. "Don't worry about it. Even you, master mediator, could never fix their beef. They'll get over it at the next get together. Lucy and Katie can be quite persuasive when they tag team them." Mateo takes his seat and leans back in it, threading his fingers together. "What can I do for you today? Not every day I get a visit from you."

I smirk and walk over to his desk. While he waits for my response, I pick up the framed picture of him and his fiancée. The little boy inside me looks for any indication on her pretty face that she's just like *him*. The monster from long ago. But her smile is bright, albeit fake. Everything about her these days is fake.

Takes one to know one, I suppose.

"I'm going to be POTUS one day," I tell him with a cocky grin.

He laughs. "So you've been telling me since you were a kid."

I set down the picture, and meet Mateo's amused stare. "I need an internship."

His brows furl together. "You're only a college freshman. Enjoy yourself a bit, son."

My shoulders tense, and I give him a slight shake of my head. Absently, I adjust my Jaeger LeCoultre Duometre Q6042422 watch on my wrist. This thing set me back over thirty grand. "You know I never enjoy myself." My words come out more bitter than I intend. Mateo is one of the few people I can be myself around, and that's a dangerous problem to have. Straightening my spine, I flash him an easy grin. "Planning for my future *is* my way of fun. You know this."

He chuckles. "I wish we had your work ethic around here. I mean, we could take you on as an intern. I'm sure the guys would be okay with that—"

"Not here," I interrupt. "Interning at Four Fathers

Freight won't help my political career." I motion to the picture on his desk. The one of him and Poppy Beckett. "Now, interning with an attorney running for lieutenant governor would. Especially considering she's the daughter of Tampa's sitting mayor. A lot of information could be gleaned from someone like her."

Understanding flickers in his eyes and he nods. Too easy, old man. Too fucking easy.

"I'll run it by Poppy tonight over dinner," he says as he stares at her picture. "And if you don't have anywhere to be, perhaps it would be better for you to dine with us." He flashes me a wicked grin. "She can't tell us no if you're sitting right there. She's too polite for that."

"She used to tell me no all the time when she'd babysit me and my brothers," I challenge.

He chuckles. "Poppy has grown up a lot since then. You're not asking to stay up past your bed time or if you can have ice cream. We're asking for a favor for the future president of the United States. We'll persuade her." His phone rings on his desk, distracting him. "My condo at seven. See you there."

I stare at the photo a second longer. Wide blue eyes. Silky blonde hair. Perfection just waiting to be destroyed. *I'm coming for you, Poppy, and you won't tell me no because I have a way of making people say yes.*

"Adam," Mateo booms into his phone. "How's my

daughter?"

I slip out of his office and walk past Trevor's office. He's muttering numbers, and it comforts me. Reminds me of Nixon. He seems preoccupied, so I walk over to the boardroom where I can hear voices. Levi and Hayden are going at it. Yelling and making threats at each other. I smirk as I keep on walking.

Dad would be so proud.

Hayden takes no shit. He's the controlling partner with majority shares. It's in his nature to remind the other partners of that every chance he gets. My brother runs FFF like a Pearson.

Unyielding. Diabolical. Powerful.

━━━━

I nod at the doorman, Ted, on my way into Mateo's building. Ted has six daughters and works two jobs just to keep a roof over their heads. The doorman job at the fancy-as-fuck condo is just a front for his side job: dealing cocaine to half the folks who live here. I know this because I know everything. You never know when you might need a favor from someone like Ted. Alibies are important. And under duress, I could make Ted vouch on my behalf if need be.

The key to power is making sure you hold all of it. Every little drop.

Once inside the elevator, I take a look at my

appearance. Dad may not have tried very hard to teach us much, but I was always watching and listening. Dad was powerful because he dressed and acted the part. Every day without fail. So each day, I don my expensive timepieces, wear my custom-made suits, and do one better than my father.

I smile.

I make them eat out of my hand because they want to, not because they have to.

That is where my dear old dad failed.

Intimidation worked for him—until it didn't. In the end, his intimidation is what got him killed by our neighbor. He pushed and pushed and pushed, never expecting to get pushed back.

But me?

I want to pull.

I want to pull everyone in and make them mine. Mine to do my bidding. Mine to control. Mine to conquer. I just want them to make that decision. Forcing them doesn't work for my agenda.

The elevator doors open with a ding. A young woman with dark brown hair and a toddler on her hip glares at me. She doesn't belong here. We both know this. Only one of us despises that fact. The other is unaffected.

I give her a slight nod and smile at the kid. He's cute and doesn't deserve to feel like an outsider. As I pass them, I rumple his hair. Maybe I'm the only person who will. Everyone needs to have their hair rumpled.

Walking down the ornate hallway, I find Mateo's unit. When I knock on the door, he wrenches it open. His lips are pursed, and he seems frazzled.

Does Poppy know her world is about to be turned upside down?

What has he told her?

He forces a smile. "Great. You're here. We were just talking about you."

"I'm often a topic of great conversation," I jest.

This time, his grin is genuine. "Come on in."

I walk past him into his home. Poppy hasn't had an opportunity to color his muted grays and whites. Ever since his daughter moved away and got married, he lives like a typical bachelor. His decorating style is much like Hayden's at the loft we share. Simple. Modern. Boring. Soon, I'll figure out how Poppy decorates her space. If it's anything like the foul-mouthed, knee-high-sock-wearing, messy-blonde-bun girl who used to babysit us from time to time, I imagine her home is filled with color.

A person can pretend all they want, but their home is where you discover who they really are.

We walk through his immaculate living room to the kitchen. Poppy, still wearing a rose-colored suit from a day at the office, stands in front of the stove. Her dirty blonde hair has been curled into prissy locks. I crave to run my fingers through them and destroy the perfection.

Soon, Cam.

Mateo, clearly on edge, clenches his jaw and frowns at Poppy. "I'll crack open some wine. Poppy, say hello to our guest." She tenses slightly, but I don't miss it. As soon as Mateo leaves the kitchen, she turns to regard me.

My, Poppy, you've turned into quite the sophisticated lady.

She doesn't smile or laugh. Not like when she'd sit on top of my kitchen island with college textbooks strewn about and her attention on her cell phone. Back then, it was a wonder how she even passed college. She spent more time yapping to her friends and planning their next outing rather than studying.

Her father must be so proud she's long since turned into *this* rather than *that*.

"You're too young for wine," she clips out in greeting, her nostrils on her pert nose flaring.

My lips tilt up on one side. I knew she'd be my biggest challenge yet. "You're no longer my babysitter."

She smooths out nonexistent wrinkles on her suit skirt. "According to Mateo, I am."

I raise a brow and lean my hip against the counter before crossing my arms over my chest. Her eyes are jerky as she skims them over me to size me up. I'm no longer the little boy who begged for attention and sweets and a motherfucking friend.

I'm Camden Pearson.

And I'm about to fuck her world.

I'm going to wring it dry and fill up my bucket with everything that was in hers.

"I can be a good boy," I tell her, flashing a wicked smile.

My dick twitches when her cheeks flame bright red. Her slender fingers come up, and she nervously twirls a strand of her hair—a mannerism I remember when she'd actually be studying. Her engagement ring, too large for her dainty finger, glimmers in the overhead light.

"I don't have time to mentor you," she says with a huff. "Mateo knows this. My plate is too full. And don't you have college courses to worry about?"

I stand up straight and take a step toward her. As though my presence alarms her, she takes a step back, her ass hitting the front of the stove. She yelps in surprise and turns the dials off.

"You don't have to teach me anything," I say lowly, letting my eyes drift down to her neck where a strand of pearls hugs her creamy flesh. "All you have to do is let me watch." Our stares meet. Hers is shocked. Mine is hot. Images of her naked and touching herself are forefront in my mind. She must read them just as I intended. Her pouty pink lips part open.

"Camden," she admonishes.

"Yes, Miss Beckett?"

She darts her gaze to the doorway behind me, her chest rising and falling with each breath she takes. "Call me Poppy," she snips. "And I haven't said yes."

I bite on the inside corner of my mouth and lift a knowing brow. "You'll say yes."

Her cheeks flame crimson once more. "You should be studying for school," she says weakly.

"I'll manage. I can handle more than one activity at once." I grin as I make a show of checking out her tits, then sliding down the rest of her body. When I look back up at her, her throat is bright red as well.

"This is...you can't..." she trails off.

"You'll let me," I rumble.

Mateo returns, carrying a bottle of wine. He raises a brow at me, and I shake my head.

"I'm not twenty-one yet," I tell him. "I'll have water."

Mateo chuckles. "I won't tell anyone."

"Nah, I'll pass."

"You're a good boy," Mateo says with a laugh.

I raise a cocky eyebrow at Poppy, loving the way her cheeks turn redder. "See? Even your fiancé agrees. Is

Monday at eight sharp okay? I can get out of class that day. You know you want to say yes."

Mateo laughs. "He's hard to tell no."

She turns abruptly to tend to the food on the stove, hiding her expressive red skin from me. "Fine. Eight sharp. I won't put up with any shenanigans."

"I'm not ten anymore, Poppy, and if I misbehave, you can punish me. Right, Uncle Teo?"

"Right," he agrees with amusement. "But he won't need punishing. Hell, soon, you'll be rewarding him. Only one of Eric's boys who ever turned out right."

"I'll have that wine now," she utters to Mateo.

TWO

P O P P Y

AFTER MY SECOND GLASS OF WINE AND A GOOD meal in my belly, I begin to relax. Only slightly, though. Camden Pearson may be all smiles and good natured, but he's a snake. Just like his father always was. Just like his older brother Hayden is. It's in their eyes. Clear as day. Camden may have been a good kid, but he's grown into something beastly.

Mateo says something to Camden that has him chuckling. My eyes skim over him now that his intense stare is elsewhere. His dark brown hair is clipped short on the sides and slightly longer on top, but he's styled it in a just-fucked way younger men pull off so easily. I'm drawn to his jawline that has been clean shaven. The bones are hard and sharp. Manly. He's nothing like the annoying kid I once babysat for. When he laughs again, I watch his pronounced Adam's apple bob in his throat. Staring at his neck, corded with muscle, is a bad idea, so I skim lower. The suit he's wearing is custom-made and expensive. It fits him perfectly. Navy blue with pale blue stitching and a matching handkerchief folded neatly in his pocket over his chest. His shoulders are broad, and I know it's from swimming. I knew from overhearing Mateo that Camden was offered swimming scholarships all over the US. And being that he was valedictorian at his high school, he had academic scholarships lined up too.

I'm still wondering why he stayed in Tampa.

Same university I went to.

Certainly not anything a presidential hopeful would want on his résumé.

"I'll grab us some more wine, angel," Mateo says as he rises from his seat. I force my eyes on my soon-to-be husband. I've known Mateo since I was a teenager. Back then, he'd been a gorgeous, albeit married at the time, man way out of my reach. I lusted over him, but knew he'd never be into someone like me.

But his wife died.

Later, my dad pushed our union.

And the rest is history.

Mateo is everything a woman could want. Handsome. Educated. Former military man. Everything he touches turns to gold, which is ironic since he proposed to "Tampa's Golden Girl." Being Marshall Beckett's daughter gave me that title long before I was ready to take it. Daddy has always guided me to be better than everyone else. Keep pushing. Keep winning.

Girls who are better suited for teaching a class about geography must turn into women.

The Becketts are not designed for normalcy. We're supposed to do extraordinary things. Teaching is normal. Running for lieutenant governor is extraordinary. Sometimes, though, I imagine where I would have ended up had Daddy not thrown a fit after college. Would I have gone to the classroom rather than the courtroom? Would I have married some nice guy and lived happily in my pretty little house with my pretty white picket fence? I certainly wouldn't have all this...

I stare down at the gigantic diamond on my ring finger.

Mateo proposed under the stars after a lovely dinner downtown last year. It was perfect and magical. I said yes. Unease trickles through me, and I quickly push it away. I said yes because I love him.

Right?

A hot, intense stare has me flustered again. I down the rest of my wine and avoid Camden's scrutinizing. I won't let this kid come into my life and have me rethinking everything after one dinner.

I love Mateo.

I love Mateo.

I love Mat—

"I'm looking forward to spending time with you," Camden murmurs, his leg extending under the table to brush against mine.

I jerk my leg toward me and press my lips together, finally chancing a look at his icy blue eyes. Those same eyes, in the form of Eric Pearson, once regarded me so knowingly. All I had to do was say yes and Eric would have pinned me against his refrigerator to fuck the daylights out of me. I could see it in his wolfish stare back then, just like I see it in Camden's.

I said no.

"I'm not," I snip out. Technically, he hasn't done anything to me. Yet. But I feel it coming.

His long fingers wrap around his water glass. Hands every bit as big as Mateo's. Images of comparing their hands side by side against my skin have me feeling flushed again. This is exactly why I don't need to work with Camden. I'm having trouble coming to terms that this beast of a man was once a little boy begging me to let him stay up so he could watch Iron Man.

I don't know the person in front of me, but I can tell he wants to know me.

Mateo strides back in and opens the wine. He reaches past me to take my wine glass and fills it up. His lips brush across the top of my head before he sits back down. I stare at my fiancé as he chats with Camden, my chest feeling hollow. He never asks me for anything, but gives me the world on a platter. It's everything a woman could want. Mateo is nice and handsome and successful.

But...

I drive away the buts that always spring into my mind.

The buts don't matter.

Camden talks politics easily with Mateo, and I find myself joining in. So much for staying away. He doesn't try to make me feel uncomfortable anymore, and eventually, I warm to having him here. After the kitchen is cleaned, we retire to the living room where I sit beside Mateo. He doesn't take my hand or hug me to him to reassure me. Normally, Mateo's lack of affection doesn't bother me, but today, I'm on edge and could use his gentle touch.

Because right now, where Mateo lacks, Camden makes up for it.

He touches me everywhere.

With his eyes and half grins.

God, just yesterday, my life was perfectly fine. I was having lunch with Daddy and discussing a speaking engagement of mine coming up. We both laughed about being way too busy to be having lunch, but we enjoyed each other's company nonetheless. Yesterday, I didn't dream I'd be so rattled by a Pearson.

I see Hayden whenever I make it up to Mateo's

office for a visit, but he's broody, and quite simply, a dick. Avoiding him is easy. The other Pearson boys are busy doing their own thing. And for the longest time, I hadn't laid eyes on Camden. Then, he shows up out of nowhere and imbeds himself in my life.

What's his play?

"Allow me to drive you home," Camden says, interrupting my inner thoughts. He rises to his full height, and I'm forced to stare at his solid, muscular thighs through his slacks.

"That would be very nice—" Mateo starts.

"I'm staying the night with you," I blurt out, shooting Mateo a panicked look.

He frowns at me, clearly uneasy about my outburst. "Your place is closer to your office. Did you even pack a bag? Fridays are hell in the courtroom. Rushing to get through traffic seems unwise."

Normally, I stay over once or twice during the weekend, but never during the week. And he never stays over at mine. Sex is a weekly occurrence, but not much more than that.

"Then come to my apartment," I plead, taking his hand.

I chance a look at Camden, and he smirks at me. Bastard.

"I'll see myself out then," Camden says. "Thank

you for dinner. I look forward to Monday." He leaves without another word.

Mateo releases my hand and stands. He plucks our empty wine glasses from the table and exits the room. I stand on wobbly legs and hurry into the kitchen. His jaw clenches as he rinses out his glasses.

"What's wrong?" I mutter, my hand resting on his shoulder.

He gives me a disapproving look, one that could rival my father's. "He's just a kid. Not his father."

I wrench my hand away from him as though I've been burned. "I wasn't trying to insult him. I just thought we could—"

"He's like a nephew to me, Poppy," he says with a huff. "You embarrassed me. Embarrassed yourself. You're acting like Eric was sitting there trying to coax you into bed."

I clutch my pearls, horrified at his words. "What?"

He shakes his head. "I'm not stupid, angel. You find him attractive. Your face burns bright red any time he's near."

"No," I croak. "I just don't like him."

"Well, regardless, he's like family to me. If you're to be my wife, you need to not act like he's about to attack you. The kid has seen shit no kid should see. His parents..." He tugs at the knot on his tie before regarding me with a grim stare. "He's dealt with enough in his lifetime. The last thing I need is for him to not feel welcome by my fiancée."

Stung by his words, I retreat and cross my arms over my chest. "I'm sorry. I didn't mean..." I trail off, fighting back tears. Mateo and I have never argued. Not once. Smooth sailing until Camden Pearson came rocking our little boat.

"We'll blame the wine," he says abruptly. "I'll call you a cab."

"I can't stay?"

He swallows and looks past me out the window. "I don't want you to."

"Mateo..."

"I'll call you a cab. Pack a bag for tomorrow, though. We'll have dinner at your favorite steakhouse."

I've been dismissed.

Chastised, I seek out my purse. As I pass him on my way out of his condo, I turn and tilt my head up to him, offering my mouth. I need the reassurance that I didn't just screw everything up by not being supportive of him and *his family*.

He bypasses my mouth and kisses the top of my head.

Not the reassurance I was looking for, but I'll take it.

"I'm sorry," I mutter.

"I know you are."

And with that, I leave.

The tears don't start falling until I've passed the doorman and stepped outside. Thunder rolls in the distance, and the wind has picked up. I find a bench and park my tipsy ass. The last thing I need is for someone to see me bordering on drunk and crying. When you're running for office, everything is used against you. And my opponent, Phil Lawton, would love nothing more than to find something to use against me.

A navy blue and chrome Bugatti Chiron pulls up to the curb and beeps the horn. Water droplets sprinkle on my face. Absently, I stand and bite back a smile. Of course Mateo would overdo it on the "cab." My heels clack on the concrete as I run over to the vehicle. The door pops open from the inside, and I'm met with luscious bright red leather interior. A strong, familiar hand adorned with a sparkly and expensive watch waves me inside.

"It's about to start pouring. Get in." Out here, under the cover of night and an impending storm, the man behind those words is not the one from upstairs.

"How do *you* have a Bugatti?" I demand, leaning down to peer inside.

He looks completely at ease inside the car that easily costs millions. "How do *you* even know what a

Bugatti is?" he challenges back, his blue eyes dark and menacing. "Get in."

"My client owns several," I snap. "And no."

He shrugs. "Suit yourself, Poppy, but you're about to get wet."

Rain begins pounding against my back. I let out a squeal and drop inside the luxury sports car, feeling gleeful I'm getting it wet. When I slam the door shut, I meet his stare with narrowed eyes. "Whatever game you're playing, I don't want any part of it. Just take me home."

He glances down at his watch, taps the glass face three times, and then reaches across me to grab the seatbelt. In his space, his scent is overwhelming. Clean and minty. A hint of cologne I have the craving to inhale. He buckles me in, then peels out away from the building without another word. I let out a squeal of surprise, and he laughs. Rich, decadent, evil.

We zip down the streets, darting in and out between cars. My heart is practically in my throat.

"You're going to wreck this million-dollar car!" I yell at him.

"Three point two and a car like this obeys his master. We're not wrecking."

I have too many questions on the tip of my tongue. I knew Eric Pearson was loaded before he died, but I didn't think his sons would have access to all that money. I want to ask him about it, but then it would mean I care.

I don't care.

"How can you afford this?" Apparently, I do care.

"Grandad bought it for my eighteenth birthday," he tells me as he jolts around a corner and zooms down another street. "My brother Hayden has one just like it."

Spoiled brats.

"Does *Grandad* know you're driving so recklessly in a car that costs more than most folks make in their lifetime?" I demand.

He ignores me and drives across town to where my building is. Once he stops and throws the vehicle into park, he glowers at me. All smiles gone. "Gifts imply that once they're given, they are no longer of the giver's concern. If Grandad isn't concerned, why the hell is little Poppy Beckett worried?"

I gape at him, my mouth parted as I will myself to shoot him a snappy retort. Nothing tumbles out. Instead, I find myself acknowledging how gorgeous he is. And young. When he reaches for me, my eyes flutter closed. Stupid wine is making me crazy and irrational. His thumb brushes along my bottom lip, sending shivers that have nothing to do with my wet clothes rippling through me.

"Close your mouth, Poppy," he growls, "before I put something in it."

I blink my eyes open at him and nearly melt in his heated glare. He pushes my chin up, closing my mouth, then releases me.

"How do you know where I live?" I ask.

"Because I know everything. See you Monday," he calls out after me.

I run from the young devil and his fancy car, thankful for the rain to cool off the heat still burning through me.

He's up to something for sure.

And I'll be damned if I let him succeed.

I'm a Beckett.

Becketts win.

We especially don't lose to a Pearson.

THREE ⸻

C A M D E N

CHARMED PROFESSOR WHARTON INTO LETTING me take my exam early. *Check.*

Charmed the receptionist at Minton, Stites, and Wells Law Firm into letting me go where I needed. *Check*.

Charmed Mateo into telling me Poppy's favorite coffee at Starbucks to earn brownie points. *Check.*

Now, I just have to charm her.

I sit across from her empty desk with my feet propped up on one end. Her coffee steams from where I set it on her coaster. We're both hot as we wait for her. I knew she had court earlier, thanks to the receptionist and her word vomit around me. Nellie is her name. Nellie is attractive, and probably my type if I were on the prowl. But I'm not looking. Her bouncy tits and flirting did nothing for me or my cock.

When I have my sights set on something, nothing pulls me away from my goal. My goal is Poppy Beckett. I'm going to fucking ruin her.

As if on cue, she rushes into the room. Her face is down as she reads something on her phone. She tosses a messenger bag to the floor and her purse hits the floor beside it with a clatter. A stress ball, a tube of lipstick, and a hairbrush all scatter from the purse. Ignoring the mess, she sits down at her desk, her brows furrowed as she reads. I'm amused when she sips the coffee I brought before tapping away on her device. It isn't until I clear my throat that she notices me in the room with her. She nearly drops her coffee, and it splashes all over her suit jacket as she struggles to catch it.

"You scared the shit out of me," she hisses, her cheeks blossoming pink the moment our eyes meet.

I smirk and nod toward her soiled jacket. "You should pay better attention."

She lets out a frustrated huff and sets down her coffee. I watch with satisfaction as she struggles to clean the coffee off her jacket with a tissue. Eventually, she gives up and pulls the jacket off. Her white button-up blouse is tight, revealing her perfect tits underneath. My cock thickens as I wonder just how long it'll take until I get her naked.

By the end of the week.

Without a doubt.

"Hey," she snaps. "Eyes up here, buddy."

Ignoring her outburst, I pin her with a knowing

stare. "How was your weekend?"

She swallows, and the fire that was just burning through her is squelched. "Fine. Yours?"

"Also fine. Went sailing with some friends."

"You know how to sail?" she asks, her nose scrunching.

I lean forward and grin. "I know how to do everything."

Her eyes fall to my lips, so I lick them for good measure. She lets out a ragged sigh before turning her attention to the screen. I watch as she types in her password: WILDHEARTS2.

"What's on the agenda, boss lady?"

"Well, for one, my name is Poppy. Two, you get to watch and watch only, remember?" Her back straightens and she purses her lips. Poppy Beckett is no longer caught off guard like she was last week or moments ago. She's found some solid ground and is ready to go toe-to-toe.

Game on, woman. Game fucking on.

"I'm watching," I rumble. "Carry on."

She's stiff for most of the day, but once she realizes I'm taking notes and not harming her, she relaxes. After several hours, she has relinquished her calendar to me. I help her prioritize her clients and her political engagements. Everything is color coded—blues, greens, grays—to indicate business appointments. Her calendar is a blur of boring. The only color is every other Saturday which is coded pink. As I get acquainted with her calendar, our eyes meet more and more over the screen. Once or twice, I even steal a smile from her.

A real smile.

Not the fake bullshit she gives everyone else.

Her office phone rings, and she takes the call. While she's distracted, I peruse through her cell phone, no longer interested in her schedule. I program my number in and text myself. I also take it upon myself to read all her texts from those closest to her. She and Mateo are about as boring as can be. An outsider would never consider them romantically involved based on their text conversations alone. In fact, an outsider would never know the real her based on her phone. Her wallpaper is a picture of a gavel. Lame. Her photo folder is completely empty. In her deleted folder, there are pictures of plants and the Tampa skyline. Even a selfie with her tongue sticking out. I text them all to me. She has emails and messages galore, but they're all business related. I can't find anything that would reflect her having a life outside of running for lieutenant governor.

"Of course," she purrs into the phone. "Mateo and I will be there, Governor. Wouldn't miss it for the world."

Fake. Fake. Fake.

While she pretends and schmoozes, I download

a porn app. Then, I look through her cookies. She looks at travel destinations a lot, not that she has time to travel. Maldives. Cozumel. Eastern Caribbean Islands. I even find where she's looked up some people from her high school through a classmates app. Of course, it's all been deleted. It's as though she tries to stamp out the zany Poppy who used to babysit my brothers and me. At twenty-nine, she's no longer that beautiful, carefree college girl.

She's this picture-perfect woman who so carefully cultivates her life for all to see.

Bored with her phone, I erase my existence from my snooping, and then set it back down on the table. Today, I wear a Carl F. Bucherer Manero watch with a chocolate leather band. I stare, fixated on the second hand as it *tick, tick, ticks* around.

"Nice watch. Grandad buy that for you too?"

I snap my stare her way and grin at her. "Not exactly."

Her cool expression fades as she searches my eyes. "Are you always so mysterious?"

"I'm not the one hiding my desire to swim naked in the ocean or my obsession with pretty flowers," I tell her smugly. "I like cars. I like watches. I like boats. End of story."

She blushes and picks at her perfectly manicured

nail, chipping at the nude polish. I remember when it used to be painted blue or pink or orange. Back when she didn't have to put on a show for others. "I don't know what you're talking about."

Little liar.

"So you're going to Governor Mike Paxton's birthday tomorrow night?" I ask, changing the subject.

Momentarily stunned, she frowns at me. "Yeah. How'd you know?"

"I overheard you talking." I gesture to her phone. "And it's on your calendar."

She rubs at her temple. "Right. Sorry. Headache."

"Too much wine last night?"

She swallows and shakes her head. "I haven't had wine since Thursday. Mateo and I both agreed I had too much."

I bite back a laugh. Does she like it when Mateo daddies her? "Noted. Stress?"

"Maybe," she admits. "Or lack of protein. And before you say anything gross, I—"

"Let's go," I interrupt as I stand. "You don't have another appointment until three. We can grab some lunch. My treat."

She stares up at me in confusion. "I don't have time to go to lunch."

"You do, and you will. Move your ass, Beckett."

"Camden!"

I squat beside her purse and shove the spilled contents back inside while sneaking a peek. Makeup. Planners and notebooks. Perfume. Nothing of interest. She's standing by the time I hand it to her. Our fingers brush, and the blush on her neck returns.

It's almost too easy.

Instead of pushing, though, I pull. Flash her a flirty smile. Let my eyes linger on her tits. Toss her a wink. She lets out a frustrated sigh, but based on the smile she fights, she likes the attention. I spent an entire evening watching her and Mateo interact, and it's almost laughable the way they are together. It makes me wonder if the old man can get her to orgasm. I'm surprised she doesn't have sex scheduled in her calendar.

Come to think of it...

"What's the pink code for every other Saturday?" I blurt out as we exit her office.

She stops and gapes at me. "W-What?"

I lift my hand and close her mouth, letting my fingers linger there. I notice Nellie watching our exchange and she quickly looks away. "Pink, Poppy. What's the pink stand for?"

She steps away from me and quickly scans the room where people are working. Instead of answering, she storms down the hall to the elevators. I trot to keep up with her. Her foot taps as she waits for the doors to open. Prowling over to her, I stand closely behind her so I can inhale her sweet scent. Lemons. I bet she tastes tart too.

Leaning forward, I bring my mouth to her ear. "Is pink for pussy? Is that something I get to watch too?"

She gasps, and before she can get away, I chuckle against the shell of her ear. The doors open, and she rushes inside. I casually look over my shoulder and grin at an older woman watching. She smiles politely at me and looks back down at her work. I follow Poppy inside the elevators and admire how flustered she is. Her arms are crossed as she faces me, her nostrils flaring with anger.

"What?"

"You can't act like that," she snaps. "I have a fiancé. You don't get to say those things to me."

I lift a brow. "What things?"

"*Those* things."

"Is pussy one of *those* things? I like *those* things if that's the case."

She swallows and looks down at her feet. "Someone could have seen or heard."

"Seen or heard what? We were simply discussing your calendar."

The doors ding open and several people enter. Taking the advantage, I sidle up next to her. She doesn't move away, but won't look me in the eye either.

"I bet Saturdays are for pussy. Does he lick you those days? Do you have such busy schedules you have to pencil in his cock?" I taunt, my voice low and only audible for her.

She lifts her chin and glowers at me. God, she really is beautiful with the fire flaming through her. "I'm not answering that for so many reasons."

"Since I'm helping with your calendar," I continue, ignoring her, "I could help you schedule in more days. And if he's too busy on those days, I could assist."

The elevator doors open again to let more people file in. She shifts away from me, and I step closer to her. My dick is hard, and I slightly press against her back to let her know, then place a discreet hand on her hip nearest the wall.

"Every day could be pussy day," I breathe against her hair. "All you have to do is say yes."

"No," she hisses.

More people file in, and I'm forced to corner her altogether. Her breathing has quickened.

"Who says no to daily pussy play, hmmm?" I nip at her ear through her hair and slide my palm from her hip to her toned stomach. Pulling her closer to me, I let her feel how she affects me.

"I'm going to kill you the moment we get off this

elevator," she warns.

My dick jolts against her.

Her threats turn me on.

FOUR

P O P P Y

H E LAUGHS AS I ALL BUT RUN TO THE PARKING garage toward his obnoxious car that takes up four parking spots. The lights flash and it beeps as he unlocks it for us. I climb into the passenger seat, and the moment he's inside with me, I lay into him.

"What the hell is wrong with you?" I screech, fury bubbling up inside me. "Anyone could have seen us!"

The smug bastard grins wickedly at me. "There's an 'us'?"

"What? No!" I peek out the windows, but don't see anyone nearby, thank God. "You're a stalker. I'm telling Mateo I can't do this anymore."

He shoves the key into the ignition and turns over the engine. "You're breaking up with him over me? Those feelings seem early, but hey, women are fickle creatures."

"I'm not breaking up with him, asshole. Stop twisting my words. You. You're out of here. Tonight, I'm telling Mateo what a pig you are."

He peels out of the parking spots and barrels out of the garage. I scramble to get my seatbelt on just as we fly out onto the main road. He pulls out some trendy sunglasses and puts them on, hiding his calculating gaze from me. I cross my arms and glare out the window. We pass several restaurants my co-workers or Mateo and I frequent, heading toward the bay. My anger for him simmers as he winds us down the roads overlooking the sparkly waters. Tension bleeds from me as I trade in my anxiety for the beauty before me. We drive into a parking lot in front of a long pier.

Snookie's Clams.

I've eaten here a few times when I was a teenager, but never as an adult. Dad would probably want to have me tested for worms if he knew I stepped into this place again. I can't imagine it could have gotten any better over the years. I'm shocked rich boy Camden chose it.

"I promised you lunch," he grits out before exiting the vehicle.

I huff out of the car after him, my high heels catching on the gravel. His hard face breaks into a smile when I wobble on the rocks, nearly tumbling to the ground.

"Careful, Beckett," he sneers. "If you fall, I'm going to catch you. And once you're in my arms, I won't let go."

I know it's a threat, but my body warms several

degrees. "What did I ever do to you?"

Ignoring me, he turns and strides over to the pier. His long legs leave me in the dust to scuttle after him like a little crab. By the time I make it to the end of the pier where the restaurant is, he's already commandeered an outdoor table.

I sit across from him and try to remain angry. My attempts fail when he chats with the waitress, telling her to bring us their specials. He orders a mixed drink for me and water for himself. The youngest Pearson is so sure of himself. I suppose money makes a man that way.

A *man*.

And, God, is he ever a *man*. So much *man*, I can't seem to ignore him like I want.

His shades sit on his perfect nose, hiding his intense blue eyes from me. Since he groped me in the elevator, I blatantly inspect him, not caring what he thinks. Joke's on me, though, because I like looking at him. He may be a smug, arrogant bastard, but he's a hot one.

Shame courses through me, and the moment the waitress hands me a drink the same blue as his eyes, I shove a straw in it and begin sucking it down. Rum. Coconut. Blue raspberry. It's good and cold and distracts me from the other delicious thing on this pier. Mateo was right. I do find him attractive. But I also hate his guts. My life was perfectly fine this time last week. Everything going as planned.

He is not part of the plan.

"Don't drink that so fast," he bites out. "I thought you had a headache."

"I do, and he's looking right at me," I hiss back.

He shoves the basket of bread across the table at me. "Eat, smartass."

Unlike when Mateo chastises me, I don't feel like I'm in trouble. Nor do I care. But I am hungry, so I grab a cheesy roll and bite on it unladylike. His lips twitch as he fights a smile.

"Feisty," he says, his grin growing as he gestures at me.

"Fucker." I wave back at him.

He throws his head back and laughs, scaring some gulls nearby. My flesh heats once again, and I blame the rum. I pick up my glass and suck more down, all the while, checking out my nemesis.

Deciding ignoring him is better, I turn my view to the bay behind him. I wonder if he sails out there or goes into the gulf. I'd ask him if he could act like a normal person, but I can't trust him not to turn it sexual. The warm breeze blows some hair into my face, and I push it away.

"Seems like a messy bun day." He leans back in his chair, resting his ankle on his knee, and motions to my hair.

I run my fingers through the slightly tangled locks and shake my head at him. "I was told messy buns reveal a messy person." Wincing, I try not to think about one of the big blowout fights I had with my father over my future.

Camden remains silent. When I look up at him, his jaw is clenched and he appears angry. I don't understand him. I hate the way he's slammed into my life and trying to mess everything up.

"I'm going to the dinner tomorrow night," he blurts out.

I frown. "The governor's?"

"Yes. You and Mateo are going to take me."

"No."

"I really like it when you say yes," he growls. "I need this connection."

His words calm me. It's not some fancy scheme to bed his old babysitter. Mateo told me all about Camden's aspirations. Meeting with Mike would be beneficial to him. Hell, maybe Mike would even take over as his mentor, relieving me from the awful task.

"I don't know," I mutter.

"Say yes, Poppy."

I exhale as more hair flies into my face. "You can't embarrass me."

He laughs. "You do that all by yourself, beautiful."

Fire flashes through me. "I was doing just fine until you came along."

"Say yes, Poppy."

"You're an ass."

"Say yes, Poppy."

I start to open my mouth, but he blurts out a question at the same time I give in to what he wants.

"Pink means sex, hmmm?"

"Yes."

He laughs again, and heat burns my cheeks. Tears prickle at my eyes. This time, when the wind blows the hair in my face, I let it hide me. I'm going to cry. Tough, hardened Poppy Beckett is going to cry in front of this rich prick.

Pink *does* mean sex. It used to not be on my calendar at all, that is, until I had to start begging for it. Mateo, while a good bed partner, doesn't initiate sex often. It's one of the only times I truly feel like I'm part of him, like we belong together, and he seems to not be that interested in it. Especially now that we're engaged.

"How's the headache?"

The voice is close. Soft. Gentle.

A sob catches in my throat.

Hot, strong fingers catch my hair, and he pushes it behind my ear. He kneels in front of me in his expensive suit, looking sorely out of place. Beautiful and caring. Not a Pearson at all.

"Open up," he mutters.

My brows furrow, but then he shows me two migraine pills. I accept the medicine, relishing the soft touch of his fingers, and then let him bring a glass of water to my lips.

This looks so bad.

Young, sexy Camden kneeling in front of his old babysitter.

If the press got a hold of this...

"Thank you," I rush out, waving him back over to his seat. "I'm fine now."

He rises and sits back down, surprisingly backing off. We eat the most delicious lunch I've had in years in companionable silence. After lunch, he tosses down several hundreds as we stand. The waitress lets out a squeal as soon as we walk away.

"Sir!" she calls out after us. "You left too much! Your bill was only fifty-two dollars."

He turns, walking backwards, and grins at her. "Keep it. Vote for me as president one day," he jests.

Her laugh is loud, carrying over the gulls and breeze. "You've got my vote, Mr. President."

He beams at me before turning to walk beside me. When we reach the end of the pier, he tosses me over his shoulder, and I scream out in surprise.

"Camden! What are you doing? Put me down!"

He playfully swats my ass as he carries me over to his Bugatti. "I'm doing you a service. Can't have you breaking your ankle on my watch, Popps."

My heart flutters for so many reasons.

Camden is trouble. Big trouble.

As soon as I get back to the office, this all needs to come to an end. If I don't stop it now, it's going to escalate into something that will blow up in my face.

FIVE ⸻

C A M D E N

I TRAIL INTO THE LE MÉRIDIEN BEHIND MATEO AND Poppy. This evening, she's exquisite in a figure-hugging white dress. Demure upon first inspection, it's cut high in the front, revealing nothing of her chest, but the back is low-cut, showing off every creamy inch. Her heels are a nude color and make her closer to my height. Long, blonde hair is curled, but she has it pulled off to one side and hanging over her right shoulder. Everything about her outfit screams sex. Too bad her personality screams dud.

Plastic smile.

Fake laughs.

Rigid back.

She plays the part so well. Politician in the making. I know because I am her. We do what has to be done to get where we want to be. She wants to be lieutenant governor. I want to be more.

She and Mateo stop to talk to the birthday boy,

and I hang back, clasping my hands together behind my back and watching passing people with smiles and nods. Eventually, they all turn to regard me, and I stride over to them.

"Mike," Poppy purrs, "meet my intern, Camden Pearson. You better watch him, he'll take your job one day."

They all laugh, and I stretch my lips into a smile. "Governor. Pleased to meet you."

We shake hands and discuss some local policies he ran on. Poppy pipes up on some of the policies she'd like to help with if she gains the lieutenant governor position. They sound rehearsed, but everyone listens with rapt attention. Five bucks says all three of us are more focused on her pouty red lips than what's coming out of them. She's in her element, though, and not giving off any vibes that she's uncomfortable. Her chin is lifted and she smiles frequently. Her blue eyes shine with focus and intensity, catching the eyes of everyone in this place. Passion looks good on her.

I watch every detail about her while not bringing attention to myself, picking up on her ticks and cues— cues I will use to my advantage—cues that will help me further my agenda when it comes to her. When she feels nervous about a topic, she starts to twist her hair, looking every bit as young as when she sat on my kitchen island attempting to figure out math problems. Beautiful. Sexy, but unsure. It's distracting as fuck. I try not to focus on her sex appeal, and instead, turn my attention to her nervous ticks. When she's feeling uneducated about a certain topic, she pretends. Always the motherfucking fake. She casts her eyes down during those moments, flutters her lashes in an innocent way, and changes the subject. They're all immune to her abilities as she steers them back into familiar territory. But I see. I see all. And, as the night wears on, I catch her rubbing at her temples at points.

All that pretending gave poor little Poppy a headache.

When she excuses herself and slips away to the ladies' room, I also take my leave, bored with Mateo and Mike discussing properties Uncle Trevor has for sale. I stride after Poppy and step into the women's restroom. Casting my gaze around, I ensure we're alone before pushing the lock into place and walking over to where she fumbles around in her clutch purse.

I reach into my pocket and hold out my palm. "Looking for these?"

She jerks her head my way, blinking in confusion. "What are you doing in here?"

"Saving your ass. Looks like I'll need to get used to doing that if I'm to spend my free time assisting you." I nod at the migraine pills in my hand. "Take these."

All the hardness in her features melts away as relief flashes in her big blue eyes. Where my eyes are icy blue with steely hints of gray hidden within, hers are the color of the ocean waters she so desperately craves to wade in. Her fingertips graze against my palm, and she shivers. As if the sensation never happened—as if I created it in my mind—she turns back to the mirror and chokes the pills down dry, gagging.

I raise a brow before gesturing toward the sink, and she scrambles to turn on the water. Moving to stand beside her, I gather her silky tresses in my grip so they don't get wet as she drinks from the faucet. When she finishes, she turns off the tap and our eyes collide in the mirror, my fingers still wrapped around her hair. It would be so easy to yank up her dress, tear her panties from her little ass, and bend her back over the sink. I'd show her what it feels like to well and truly get fucked.

"You can let go now," she breathes, her lashes fluttering. She doesn't want me to, though. Her eyes plead with mine, and she probably doesn't even realize it.

"I don't want to." My lips quirk up on one side. Flirtatious. Playful. I will let go of her. I won't fuck her. But she doesn't need to know all my cards. "I really don't want to." When I step closer, pressing my cock against her back, she lets out a mewl.

"Camden..."

I press a soft kiss to her exposed neck before letting her hair go. She remains frozen as I adjust the locks back into their original position off to one side. She clutches the strand of pearls around her neck, another nervous move, and I stifle a smirk.

One day, I'll give her a pearl necklace...

"Pearls," I say lowly. "I imagined you as more of a sapphire girl." Like her eyes. Like her motherfucking birthstone. Like the fun, chunky fake jewelry she wore as a college kid. Now, she's a pearl-clutching bore.

"They were gifts," she mutters, backing away from me. It's cute how she thinks distancing herself in the small bathroom will keep me away.

I track her with my eyes, drawing the same effect as my touch without not needing to touch her to have the same effect. Her flesh is red, and I fucking love it. "From your fiancé?" I taunt.

Her plump lips press together. "And my father."

Bang! Bang! Bang!

With a wink, I turn, unlocking the door, and she rushes into a stall just as I open it. A pretty brunette goes from being annoyed to batting her eyelashes in a matter of seconds.

"I think you've stepped into the wrong bathroom," she says before biting on her bottom lip.

"My mistake," I rumble. "Would you be a doll and show me to the right one?"

I offer my arm, she takes my elbow, and away we go.

———

"You're home late," Hayden grunts from the sofa, his girlfriend Katie sleeping with her head in his lap. He changes the station to the news and nods at the recliner beside him.

I shed my tuxedo jacket and yank off my bowtie before settling in the chair. Schmoozing with some of the biggest players in this city wasn't difficult. That shit is second nature to me. Fucking with Poppy? Easy.

It was *him.*

Seeing *him* was fucking difficult.

"Everything okay?" my brother asks. "You're not acting like yourself."

I flash him an easy grin. "Just thinking about a girl." Not a total lie.

Hayden snorts. "Better than a guy."

If Nixon were here, he'd knock Hayden on his ass for that comment. It's not like Hayden knows how much it bothers me, though. My mind drifts to my early teenage years.

Am I gay?

It's a question that eats me alive each day. That man

did those things to me. Did he see something I don't?

I open my Tumblr app and look up gay porn. My dick doesn't twitch. If anything, I start to sweat and get that creepy feeling that sometimes shudders down my spine as I remember him. *It's not that these people are grossing me out. It's what* he did. *It's how* he made me feel. *Bile rises in my throat as a familiar panic attack rears its ugly head. I breathe in and out, trying desperately to slow my racing heart.* He didn't give me a choice. He *didn't ask.*

I quickly exit the search and go back to the stuff that does get my dick hard. Blonde-haired beauties with jiggly tits and smooth pussies. My cock rises, and I let out a breath of relief. I'm not gay. Nothing against them, but I prefer women.

"Dude," Hayden says softly, jerking me from my memory. "I'm just kidding. You know I love you no matter what. Brock's bi and we support that shit."

I laugh, but it feels hollow. "I'm fine. Just tired. I've got an early morning. I'm going to head to bed."

"Class or your new internship?"

Rising to my feet, I stretch and yawn. "I have to run in and turn in an assignment, but then I'll be at the law firm." With little perfect Poppy.

"I'm here to talk. If you ever need me," Hayden says, his tone serious. "I'm not your dad, but I'm your big brother. I can help you if you're ever in trouble or need to talk."

I groan. "Are you about to start your period, man?"

He throws a couch pillow at me, but I dodge it. "Fuck off, kid," he shoots back, smiling. Hayden is much happier these days. His girl has changed him for the better. When she finally moved into our loft, my brother began smiling more and lightening the fuck up. Katie is good for him.

Speaking of her...

It's now or never.

"I'm moving out."

Hayden's smile falls. "What the fuck? Why?"

"Because it's time, Hay."

He eases her head out of his lap and stands before stalking my way to grip both my shoulders. "No." Stubborn as fuck this brother of mine.

Gently, I push him away from me. "Yes. Then, you can have the alone time you two desperately need. To plan weddings and make babies and shit."

"We're not exactly making babies and shit. This condo is big enough for the three of us," he says, practically fucking pouting.

Not making babies, but planning a wedding for sure. Or at least soon. I went with him to pick out the giant rock he plans to give her. It won't be long. "I know," I say with a sigh. "And I'll be over here all the time to eat because we all know I can't cook for shit. I just want my own place."

He spears his fingers through his hair and scowls. "I don't know..."

"It's not your decision. You're not my guardian anymore. I'm an adult and have my own money. I need to do this, okay?"

Reluctantly, he nods. "Fine, but I expect you over for dinner every weekend, asshole."

"As long as I don't have to watch you and Katie make out, it's a deal." I grin.

He grumbles, and I leave him to call my other brother. Dropping onto my bed, I dial Nixon. He picks up on the first ring.

"Yo," he grunts.

"What's up?"

"Just watching my girls sleep."

"That's creepy," I utter.

He laughs. "One day, you'll get it. It's not fucking creepy, I know that much."

"I'm moving out."

"Do we need to make up the guest room?"

I shake my head. My brothers are more of a father than mine ever was. They make up for where he lacked. "Not with you, dick. On my own."

"Tampa?"

"Yep. You can't get rid of me that easy."

"I'm not ready to lose you to DC yet," he says, chuckling. "Plus, a kid will need his uncle."

"You know, I'm technically Erica's brother."

"But Erica's baby brother is still your nephew."

A pregnant pause fills the line.

"Wait...are you and Rowan expecting?"

He chuckles, sounding happy as fuck. "She wanted to wait to tell anyone until we knew the sex."

"Congratulations, man," I say, grinning. "Way to spread that Pearson seed everywhere."

He snorts. "You just keep your seed to yourself for the time being. We don't need you getting distracted, Mr. President."

My thoughts drift to Poppy in her form-fitting dress and swollen red lips.

"I'm laser-focused on my goals," I assure him.

And when I destroy them, I'll get back on track with what I was born to do.

Take over the world.

SIX ──────────

POPPY

'M FRAZZLED AS I RUSH INTO MY OFFICE. FRIDAYS are hell. The judge was being difficult, and I felt like a newbie in the courtroom, scrambling to justify my evidence. It was all solid, of course, but Judge McNamara has a way about making you second guess yourself. She's older and resembles a hawk. I swear, she enjoys tearing poor little attorneys apart and eating them for breakfast.

"Calendar is up," a familiar deep voice says. "You had a phone call with a campaign donor scheduled for noon—"

Shit!

"Oh no," I groan as I drop my messenger bag and purse to the floor. "That was ten minutes ago."

Camden smiles warmly at me. He's made himself comfortable in the chair across from my desk looking all too good in his three-piece suit. The guy dresses better than the partners at this firm. "That's why I took the liberty to call and reschedule. I booked a lunch with him next week instead. He was thrilled to have more of your time than a simple phone call."

My heart races as I mentally think over my schedule for next week. "Do I even have any lunches open?"

"I sent your father an email canceling. You can meet with him anytime. Mr. Booker is now in Tuesday's slot," he tells me. "Coffee is hot. Sit. Chill out. You have the rest of the afternoon free of appointments. Then, at five, you have a meeting with your wedding planner."

I plop down in my chair and let out a heavy sigh. The last thing I need right now is to be planning a wedding. Jacque demands my focus at these wedding meetings and I'd rather be anywhere but picking out venues, flowers, and cake flavors. Mateo says it's the woman's choice, therefore he's leaving it all up to me. Since he's been married once before, he wants me to have it exactly the way I want.

The way I want is just the two of us on an island with our toes in the sand and God as our only witness. That's not so difficult. When I mentioned it to Mateo, he laughed as if my suggestion was a joke.

"Keep frowning like that and you'll get wrinkles," Camden teases.

I rub at my temples, feeling another migraine coming on. That makes one every day this week. The stress is really beginning to weigh on me. I hate to admit it, but Camden came at exactly the right time. He still undresses me with his eyes at every turn, but he's incredibly smart and takes initiative. He puts out fires with ease and keeps me on track. He's barely been here a week and I already feel like I would drown without his assistance. When I admitted that last night over dinner, Mateo had been overjoyed.

Lifting my gaze, I watch Camden as he taps away on his laptop. I know he works on assignments when I don't need him immediately. It's fascinating how he multitasks effortlessly. I'm trying to take a page from his book, but he makes it seem so simple.

"Stare too long and you might fall in love," he flirts.

I laugh, no longer angered by his advances. "I don't have time to fall in love."

His brows lift. "But you're already in love, so that doesn't matter anyway, right?"

My face heats as I realize I admitted something I hadn't yet admitted to myself. I love Mateo. I love Mateo. I love Mateo. But I'm not *in* love with him. My head throbs, and I squeeze my eyes shut. His chair squeaks, and then his palm is on my back. He strokes his fingers through my hair, and instead of yelling at him or removing myself from his touch, I allow this moment of comfort.

"When my sister-in-law was pregnant, she was

susceptible to migraines," he utters softly. "I was the only one who could help. Once, I read up on acupuncture and pressure points." His fingers dance along my skull, sending shivers through me. He begins pressing into parts of my head, temples, and neck, and I drop my head forward. Some spots do nothing. Others make me see stars. And certain areas keep the throbbing at bay.

I moan in relief, my hand clutching his wrist to keep him still. "Right there. Don't stop, Camden."

He kneads the flesh with expert hands, and I relax. It feels good. Too good. It makes me wonder what else he's good at. Heat floods through me, and I feel myself blushing again. I moan again, this time having nothing to do with my headache and everything to do with my dirty fantasies. The more I work with him, the more frequent they come. Just this morning, I got myself off in the shower, imagining it was him doing it instead. Then, guilt overcame me.

As Camden presses into my skull with his right hand, his left strokes my hair away from my neck, massaging the tightness out of my shoulder. It feels so good, I moan in relief, then panic slightly that he's going to make fun of me. Camden doesn't, though. He remains silent, and I'm thankful. If he were razzing me or flirting, I'd freak out, and I'm enjoying this moment. I selfishly don't want to be stolen from it. When he slides my suit jacket off one shoulder, I tense, but it gains him access over my blouse to work the area better.

Hot breath tickles my hair near my ear as he whispers, "Feeling better?"

"Much," I choke out. I grip my hand tighter around his right wrist, willing him to continue doing what he's doing.

He chuckles, and it vibrates straight to my core. My thighs clench, and I'm embarrassed at how wet my panties are. All from a simple massage. Thank God I'm spending the night with Mateo and can take my sexual frustrations out on him. His thumb peels back my blouse at the neck, grabbing my bra strap along the way, exposing my neck and shoulder. I let out a gasp of surprise, but then his hot hand is directly on my flesh.

We need to stop.

This feels too good. It's going to lead to things I can't undo.

And yet...

"You have so much tension," he murmurs, the heat of his words against my ear. "I'm going to work it all out."

His fingers slide lower down the front of my chest beneath my blouse, and my breath stills. I can't find the words to tell him to stop, part of me hoping he'll touch my breast. His long fingertips skim over the top, tickling me.

Don't stop.

Don't stop.

Don't stop.

God, don't stop.

"Stop," I choke out. "You have to stop."

His fingers pause, caressing my flesh just above the cup of my bra before he drags his hand up in a slow retreat. My skin burns in his absence, and I hate that I can't have what I want.

"Miss Beckett—oh...oh my," a voice says as the door to my office opens.

Horrified at our position, I swivel away in my chair to right my shirt. Camden wisely strides away from me toward Nellie.

"That looked worse than it was," he tells her. "I know how pretty little girls like to gossip. She has a migraine." He smiles as he tugs on a strand of her hair. "Plus, I don't want you thinking I'm interested in her..." he trails off, "because I've been wanting to ask you out all week."

He has?

"You have?" she breathes, her eyes wide with awe.

"Tonight. Dinner at Zaggato's?"

"The waiting list is months in advance," she utters.

"I always get what I want, Nellie. Tell me your number and I'll get your address later to pick you up at seven."

She rattles off her number, and he plugs it in his phone. I'm composed by the time they finish.

"Miss Beckett, your father called. He says the lunch you canceled was important," she finally says, smiling. "Please call him back."

"Of course," I say tightly. "And next time, knock please."

She gives me a clipped nod and Camden a bright smile before slipping from my office. The migraine is in full force now. Tears burn at my eyes. That was so close. Shit.

"Calm down, Poppy," Camden grumbles. "It was nothing. I fixed it." He reaches into his pocket and hands me a couple pills. I toss them back and swallow them dry.

"Thank you," I finally say.

"Come on. You missing lunch is a thing of the past. We'll grab food really quick. Let's go."

I rise to my feet and grab my purse. "We can't...uh, we can't ever do stuff like that. It looks bad."

"Yeah, we'd hate for Daddy to find out," he says as he storms out of my office.

What the hell?

"Camden!" I call out as I rush behind him. Several eyes dart our way, but I ignore them. He's at the elevators by the time I catch up. I grip his elbow. "What's wrong?"

He flashes me a wide smile, but his steel-blue eyes are hard. This is the look I struggle with so much. Camden Pearson is better at faking than I am. A monster lives inside him and rages to be set free. Just then, his monster was nearly cut loose.

"You can't be mad at me for what didn't happen," I say lamely. "I'm engaged."

He chuckles. "And I'm about to go on a date tonight with a beautiful woman. Nothing happened, and nothing will."

My head throbs. I don't understand his abrupt mood swing. The doors open, and I follow him inside. He mashes the button and ignores me the whole way down. Once in the parking garage, he stalks over to his Bugatti. One of the partners admires it as he climbs out of his Porsche. He gives me a nod before walking inside, leaving us alone. Camden climbs in, and I hurry after him. The tires peel out, and I quickly click my seatbelt into place.

We drive out of the garage into the sunlight. It warms my flesh, and I yawn, suddenly exhausted. Closing my eyes, I rest for a moment.

———

"A little too much to drink," Camden says. "She needs to sleep it off."

"Sleeep," I slur and giggle.

The man laughs, shaking his head. "A little early in the day for that, miss. But your secret is our secret. Enjoy your stay."

———

Migraines are the worst. I wake, thankful to realize it's gone. Squinting, I try to make sense of where I am. I'm stretched out in a bed, not a car. A very soft bed. It's dark, and I can't see anything but shadows.

Mateo's.

I'm at Mateo's.

It's all coming back to me.

It's Friday, and it's evening. That's where I am.

A warm hand caresses my stomach, and I let out a sigh of relief. I'll have to call the doctor. Losing half my day to a blackout migraine is scary. What if I have a brain tumor or something? The terror bleeds away as desire pools in my belly. Mateo's hand finds my bare breast, and he squeezes. His mouth starts pressing kisses down the middle of my chest. I moan when he spreads my thighs apart. He's rougher than usual, his fingers bruising my flesh, and I love it. His body presses against mine, his hard length straining against his boxers between us. A thrill of pleasure shoots through me as he grinds his cock against me. Almost painfully so.

I'm dizzied by his touch. My nails scrape along his flesh as he dry humps me. His lips find my neck below my ear and my back arches, pressing my tits against his chest. He smells good. Different. He smells like...

I freeze.

Panic stutters through me.

I feel his smile on my neck. "Did you enjoy your nap, Popps?"

Camden.

Oh. My. God.

"No..." I choke out.

"That's not what you were saying hours ago when I fucked you," he taunts.

I shove him hard, and he rolls off me. My body falls to the floor with a thud in my attempt to escape him. Tears spring to my eyes as I blindly search for a lamp or something. Before I can find one, the overhead light comes on. I spin around to find a disheveled Camden watching me with narrowed eyes, all flirtation and ease gone from his features.

He's glaring. Angry. His nostrils flare. His jaw clenches. Against my better judgment, I skim down his cut, muscled chest down to the dark trail of hair on his lower abs leading below his black boxer briefs. I blink several times at the way his large cock strains in his underwear—underwear smeared with my arousal across the front.

"Fuck!" I hiss. "How did this happen? What did we

do?"

He skims his gaze along my naked flesh. "What *didn't* we do is a better question."

I shake my head in horror. "No. I don't believe it."

"Oh?" He saunters over to the bedside table and pulls out his phone. "This says otherwise." He tosses it on the bed between us.

Dread pools in my belly.

I snag the sheet from the bed and wrap it around me, hiding my nakedness from him, then snatch up the phone. It's open to his pictures folder. I stare in disbelief.

There we are. Middle of the day. Lying in the bed. Naked. My eyes are closed, and his lips are on mine as he takes a selfie.

No.

No.

No.

When I flip through the pictures, I'm stunned to find several of them with us in intimate positions. I recall nothing. Holy shit.

"Did you rape me?" I ask, horrified.

He laughs scornfully. "Nope. What you see in those pictures is all that happened."

"Why did you do this?" I start deleting pictures as quickly as I can, and he makes no moves to take the phone from me.

"Insurance."

"Insurance for what?" I screech.

He shrugs. "To get what I want."

"Which is what? To ruin my life?"

"Nobody has to know about this. Unless you decide to change things. Then, *everyone* will know," he says simply as he prowls my way.

An affair on my fiancé with my young intern. The press would have a field day and my campaign would be ruined. All I've worked for would go down the toilet.

He's blackmailing me.

Shit!

I stumble away from him as reality sets in, dropping the phone to the carpet. He backs me against the wall, tearing the sheet away. When his body presses against my bare flesh, I shudder. My eyes close as I wait for the tears that never come. My mind is too busy trying to plan how I'll fix this—how I'll erase it all. Strong, warm hands grip my hips, and I snap my gaze up to stare into his cruel blue eyes.

His thumbs rub circles along my naked skin, and I curse the way my body heats to his touch.

"What did you give me? You drugged me," I accuse, pressing my palms against his sculpted chest to push him away. He's like an immovable wall.

"A little bit of this. A little bit of that. Something

to make you sleepy. Something to make you horny." His lips curl up into an evil smile that shouldn't look hot. "You were horny first, for the record. Then you tired yourself out." He reaches up and grips my jaw in an owning way. "Do you remember the way you came all over my tongue, Popps?"

"No. I would never," I snap. But that's a lie. Memories from this afternoon flutter into my mind.

"Please," I beg. His hot breath on my naked thigh drives me wild. This is a bad idea, but for the life of me, I can't seem to figure out why. All I know is I want him.

"Say it again," he mutters, his voice husky.

"Please."

His tongue runs along my slit, and I lose my mind to pleasure.

My body heats several degrees at his touch and the memory fresh in my mind. My nipples harden as I allow myself to consider the fact that this wolf in sheep's clothing was between my thighs. And I begged him for it. *Fuck*.

"Is that so?" he murmurs. His lips press to mine, and I taste me, confirming his words.

Shit!

What have I done?

SEVEN

C A M D E N

I PUSH MY TONGUE INTO HER MOUTH, SWIPING IT across hers. She's frozen, and I take advantage, kissing her like she's never been kissed before. Hard. Punishing. I fuck her mouth like I'm going to fuck her pussy one day. And I will.

Poppy Beckett will give me everything.

She'll say yes because she has to. There is no other way.

While she's stunned and coming to terms with our arrangement, I grab her round ass and lift before sliding my palms beneath her thighs, spreading her for me. The moment my cock presses against her heat, she moans.

Too easy, Poppy.

I rock my hips against her, loving the way her breath hitches each time I press against her clit. Her pussy is drenched—thanks to the ecstasy still running through her veins—and she claws at my shoulders.

"Let me go," she moans against my mouth. "I hate

you."

I laugh as I press kisses along her jaw to her ear. "Hate can be just as hot as love."

It doesn't take much effort before Poppy comes apart at my touch. Her head bumps against the wall, and she screams with pleasure. I don't give her time to recover before I drop her to her feet and walk away. When I glance over at her, she looks like a delightful mess. Her chest rising and falling as she pants. Hair wild. Cheeks crimson. If I weren't so controlled in my plan, I'd walk right back over there and fuck her like she wants.

Oh, and does she want.

Her blue eyes blaze with lust. Swollen, pink lips part. Hell, she's not even hiding her nudity from me. Every creamy curve is on full display. One day, I'll nip and suck on every part. One day. Just not today.

"I don't understand what you want from me," she mutters, her arms crossing over her chest to try to hide herself from me.

Too bad I've seen it all, sweetheart.

"Get dressed. I'll fill you in on the way home."

She blinks at me and shakes her head. "I'll call a cab."

I pick up her discarded skirt and toss it on the bed. "No, you won't. I wouldn't go through all this trouble without reason. Get dressed and let's go. Move your ass, woman."

Fire blazes in her stare, but the tears never come. I'm thankful. Poppy was always a good target because she is strong. Most women would be a blubbering mess. I need her to remain rigid. I want to break her—and nobody wants to break something soft.

She dresses quickly, then starts hunting for something. I throw on my clothes and hold up her phone.

"Looking for this?"

She glowers at me. "Mateo must be worried sick." She looks over at the bedside clock and shudders. "It's eleven. I was supposed to come over after my appointment with the wedding planner that I missed. I'll bet he's sent out a search party by now."

I almost feel bad for her.

"Actually," I reveal with a wicked grin, "he never even texted."

Her lashes flutter as her brows crash together. "Whatever. He's worried sick."

"He's not."

I offer her phone in the palm of my hand. She storms over to it, trying to take it, and I seize the opportunity to pull her against me. Her mouth pops open in shock when I grab a handful of her ass.

"He never called or texted," I say again. "How does that make you feel?" I'd expected him to worry, and when he didn't reach out, it made my job easier.

Her nostrils flare, and the tip of her nose turns pink. She chooses this moment to burst into tears. My chest feels tight, but I ignore it. I release her and give her back her phone. She frowns as tears roll down her cheeks, all the while looking for evidence he tried to make contact. Then, she finds what I want her to.

"What's this?" she chokes out.

"The start of our illicit affair," I say, chuckling.

From the moment I got her in my car this afternoon and she passed out—thanks to the sleeping pill I'd given her in place of her migraine medicine—I texted back and forth between our phones. Documented how the affair started the night of the governor's birthday party. How we hooked up in the bathroom. That the secrets are too hard to keep from everyone. Some of the same pictures she deleted on my camera roll had been texted between us. Basically, an entire day of communication from us.

"You asshole," she snaps. "All this for my pussy?"

Shaking my head, I open the door and usher her out of the hotel room. "Don't flatter yourself, Popps. Your pussy is just a perk of our arrangement."

———

She ignores me the entire way to her apartment. This time, I park and follow her inside. I expect a fight, but she's still groggy from the medicine. Once inside her place, she motions to the couch before disappearing into her room. The shower turns on, so I make myself at home. Just as I knew, her home is colorful and fun. Plants line the windows. The walls are painted in pretty reds, oranges, and yellows. It's all very Bohemian and unlike Poppy. The girl who lives outside these walls is pastel and a fucking bore. The girl who lives within them is colorful and fun.

While she showers, I scrounge around in her refrigerator. Finding some leftovers that don't look old, I set to microwaving them for her since she hasn't eaten. Earlier, while she slept, I took Nellie to dinner like I promised. The girl practically threw herself at me in the car after, trying to kiss me. I told her when I really like someone, I like to take it slow. She seemed unsure how to take my words. And when I dropped her off, she tried to reel back in the fact that she was ready to whore herself out to me and pretended to be demure. Batted her lashes. Smiled prettily. Asked me to call her.

I deleted her number.

Nellie was just an alibi.

My phone buzzes in my pocket, and I'm thrilled to see it's one of my college buddies, Cronk. Cronk isn't his real name, but his real name is unimportant. It's what kind of friend he is that is important. Cronk is a hacker.

Cronk: Your request has been completed. I

wish I could bleach my eyeballs. You owe me, fucker.

And I do—which is why I wire him eighty thousand for his troubles, instead of the forty promised. He'll send me a "receipt" for a small yacht so it'll look legit to the IRS if they ever come sniffing around. You can never be too careful.

Me: See some old guys in speedos at the beach?

Cronk: Four of them. Filthy as fuck.

The information Cronk has uncovered will be saved to a flash drive and mailed to Nixon under the guise of a birthday present for me. Nixon will unknowingly keep it until I need it. The information will be safe.

Pocketing my phone, I walk into the living room, set Poppy's food down on a pile of magazines, then locate some wine. I bring the bottle and a glass. She's going to need it. I settle myself in the middle of the couch to wait for her. A few moments later, she stomps in looking closer to my age than her own. For a second, I'm caught by how gorgeous she is when she's being the real Poppy Beckett. Her wet hair is pulled into a messy bun. The makeup on her face has been scrubbed clean. She wears a sweatshirt several sizes too big and some tight yoga capris. My dick twitches in appreciation.

I pat the cushion beside me. "Come eat, beautiful."

She scowls, but obeys. *Good girl.* Her body settles beside mine and she gobbles up her food. As she finishes,

I pour her some wine. I watch with amusement as she guzzles it down. So petulant. It makes me want to spank her. With a smile, I pour her another glass.

"Careful," I say lowly. "If you lose your senses again, I will take advantage. It's in my nature. This time, rather than my tongue, it'll be my dick inside you."

Her pale cheeks redden, and she flips me off. "Go to hell."

"I want meetings with some influential political players," I tell her, cutting straight to the chase. When I rattle off the names of the police commissioner, the mayor, a senator, and a judge, she frowns.

"All this because you want to meet with them? For what? To have a flawless résumé?" Her voice is shrill. "You're a sociopath."

I laugh and shrug. "I think the term you're looking for is psychopath. And my reasoning is unimportant to you. All you have to do is obey."

"Or what?" she challenges, her nostrils flaring.

"Or I expose your illicit affair to every news and media outlet in the country."

"People have affairs all the time," she bites out. She downs the rest of the wine and wisely sets the glass on the table.

"But most of them are with consenting adults."

"As are we," she screeches, her face turning red

with anger.

"But what about when you were my babysitter, Poppy?"

She blinks at me in horror. "Gross. I would never... don't even insinuate something so sick."

My mind floods with my own *sick* past. It strengthens my resolve. "The media would have a field day with that. Your opponent would crucify you with that information."

"Why do you hate me so much?" she asks, her voice cracking as more tears well in her eyes. One spills out and races down her pink cheek.

I reach up and swipe it away with my thumb. "You're just a tool with a purpose."

Stars glitter in my vision when she slaps me. "Fuck you."

Gripping her throat, I push her down onto the couch, pinning her beneath me. Her eyes are wide, but she doesn't fight me off. My hand relaxes, and I use my other one to stroke her cheek. "That's the other part of our agreement."

"What?"

"If you don't get me the meetings I need within one week, we will officially begin our affair."

"I won't have sex with you. Not willingly."

I smirk at her. "You will. I could fuck you right now

and you'd be okay with it."

Her eyes narrow. "I'll tell Mateo everything."

"He won't believe you. He already puts up with you. You're a child to him. A pretty little plaything who looks good on his arm."

More tears leak from her eyes. "I'll break up with him. Then your threats will mean nothing."

I lean forward and kiss her pink nose. "Even if you broke up with him, you'll still do what I say. You want to be lieutenant governor and keep your name from getting smeared."

"I can handle a little heat," she challenges.

"There is so much more you can't handle, Poppy. So much more. And if I were to show you, you'd fucking die of mortification. Don't make me ruin you publicly. I would fucking delight in it, understand? Don't push me. You do as I say, I delete everything and go away."

"Just like that?" she breathes.

I run my thumb over her lips. "Just like that."

"When I get you those meetings, I want you gone from my life."

"My pleasure. Your life is the last place I want to be."

I press a kiss to her pouty lips, and then release her. She remains lying on the sofa staring up at me in confusion as I rise and head for the door.

"One week, Poppy."

EIGHT

P O P P Y

I WAKE WITH THE SUN BLINDING ME. MY HEART stutters to see the curtains wide open—curtains I keep closed for this very reason. It's then it all comes back to me.

Camden.

The hotel. The pictures. The blackmail.

A groan rumbles from me as I reach for my phone. I hit my emails first and check for anything important. Being that it's Saturday, there's nothing much. I'm disappointed to find no texts or missed calls from Mateo.

My heart sinks as I text him.

Me: Don't worry about me. I'm okay.

It's a childish text and Mateo will be annoyed by it, which is part of the reason I sent it. I want him to realize I'm hurt he hasn't even cared that I didn't come over or call. With a huff, I shower and dress for the day. Normally, Mateo and I spend our Saturdays when we're able touring museums or dining in the city or seeing a theater show. When the evening winds down, he takes me to bed, and I spend the rest of the evening clutching onto him. He's not exactly the comforting type, but I take what he gives, even if it is small. I check my phone, only to be disappointed again.

He doesn't respond, but someone else does.

Camden: My tongue still tastes like your sweet cunt.

I gasp in horror.

Me: You little asshole. Leave me alone.

Camden: You'll warm to the idea of anal. Trust me.

Me: What?! That's not what I meant. Stop stalking me.

Camden: Open your door.

Dread mixed with a little flutter of butterflies sends my emotions into turmoil. I hate him. I hate him. I hate him. Yet, I'm storming over to the door to let him in, heat flooding through me. Before I open the door, I take a steadying breath and push out any silly anticipation at seeing him.

The moment I see him, all pep talks are squashed and I stand there gawking. He wears a pair of charcoal gray slacks that hug his muscular thighs and are cinched at the waist with a black leather belt. His crisp, pale blue dress shirt is tucked in, and he's not wearing his usual tie. The shirt fits him in such a way, it accentuates his shoulders and biceps, making the material slightly tug over his muscles. But it's not his appearance that holds me captive, it's his smirk.

Deadly. Ruthless. Calculating.

"Here," he says, his deep voice causing the hairs on my arms to stand on end. "You'll need this."

He hands me a coffee and steps past me into my apartment. Stupid me checks out his ass when I should be beating it instead.

"When are my meetings?" he asks, darting his sharp stare to mine.

Caught looking at his ass, I blink away my daze and scowl. "I haven't made them yet."

"Time's running out." His features are impassive. Emotionless. "Call them now."

I grit my teeth and huff. "Anything to get you out of my hair."

He chuckles as I set down my coffee and pull my phone from my jeans pocket. Still no missed calls from Mateo. My anger is replaced by concern. It's not like him to just not respond. I scroll through my contacts and find Judge Knutson's number. One good thing about Camden's list of meetings is they're all people I know and have a relationship with. I can set up these meetings and get him out of my life.

As the phone rings, Camden makes himself comfortable on the middle of the sofa while I pace.

"Little Poppy," Judge Knutson says, a smile in his voice.

"Judge," I greet.

"Peter," he admonishes. "You're to call me Peter, young lady."

I laugh and try not to make eye contact with Camden. "Okay, Peter, I need a favor."

"A favor, hmmm? Is this kind of favor going to get me in trouble with the missus?" he asks, ever the flirt.

"No. It's for my intern. He wants to meet you," I reply. "This week."

"Call my assistant and set it up. I'm sure I have a few openings. We should schedule a lunch one day too," he says. "I haven't seen you in ages."

"I'll see what I have open," I lie. My week is way too busy to shoot the breeze with Peter Knutson as he eye-fucks my tits.

"Perhaps another time," he suggests.

"Of course."

We hang up, and I grin at Camden. "Good news. We just have to set it up and then..." I trail off at his expression. His steel-blue eyes are hard and unforgiving. When they lock on mine, I see into the depths of him. Bitter. Hateful. Angry.

Soulless.

The word is like a cold slap to the face. A reminder. This man is blackmailing me.

"Next," he says, his tone bored as he schools his expression into one of cool indifference.

I spend the next half hour nailing down two more meetings before dialing Dad last. He picks up on the first ring.

"Morning, sweetheart."

"Morning, Dad." My chest feels tight, and I have the urge to sob to him. If anyone knows about people using him for their political gain, it's my father. But knowing what's at stake keeps me biting my tongue. I want to be lieutenant governor, and if I can't handle a pesky man-boy who likes using his old babysitter as a political stepping stone, how the hell am I going to help run state-level responsibilities?

"I'm making my famous pot roast this evening if you and Mateo would like to stop by."

I let out a heavy sigh. "Rain check on dinner. I do need a favor, though."

"What sort of favor?" His voice turns from friendly to stern.

Most dads would simply tell their daughter yes, no matter what it was. My dad has conditions. Clearly.

"My intern needs to meet with you for school."

When I fib the last part, Camden's brow shoots up. I hate that he shows an interest in me lying to my dad. "This week."

"No can do."

Panic rises up inside me. "Dad, please."

"I have meetings all week," he grunts. "Is that all? I need to get some work done."

"It's Saturday," I huff.

"Goodbye, Poppy."

When he hangs up on me, I gape at Camden in shock.

"Daddy tell you no?" His eyes narrow and his jaw clenches. "If it were so easy, I'd have lined these meetings up myself. The fact that you got the first three is pleasantly surprising. I knew you'd have to work at this."

"You'll get your meeting," I growl. Truth is, though, I don't know if I can make that happen. Dad seemed firm on the phone, and when he says no to something, he doesn't budge. Fuck. "Even if I have to tell him my reputation is at stake."

"You can't tell him that," he snaps. When I flinch at his sudden response, he cracks his neck and relaxes. "I would rather you not," he amends.

Okay.

What the hell?

"I will have to work on him. In the meantime, you

need to leave, because I need to go check on Mateo." I rise from the sofa and hunt down my purse.

"I'm coming with you." His heat sears me as he stands too closely. "I'm going everywhere with you from now on."

I spin around, fire igniting within me. "No. You're already creeping on my life enough as it is."

His palms grip my hips and I let out a sharp breath of air. He steps until our bodies are touching. "We'll take my car."

I tilt my head up to glower at him, but it's a big mistake. Up close, in the daylight, he's more handsome than ever. And I can smell him. Minty and clean. He reaches up and gently clutches my throat before pulling me until his forehead rests against mine.

"We'll take my car," he murmurs again, his hot breath tickling my face.

It would be wise to move away from him, but I feel like a rabbit caught in a trap. Snared. His hungry stare on me. "No."

"I like it when you say yes."

He pulls away, and I'm left shivering from the loss. Damn him. I hate that wicked look in his stare. The one that enjoys screwing with my mind.

"You're an asshole," I snap.

"I am," he agrees. "It's a damn shame you're

attracted to them. Makes my job a whole lot easier."

━━━━━━

He's quiet as he follows me down the hallway to Mateo's condo. I'd rather it be this way. If he's going to loom over me like a plague-carrying creep, at least I can ignore him if he doesn't speak. It's when he talks that I lose my mind. He says things just to push my buttons. So easily he's able to push them.

"You're huffing," he observes.

I shoot him a withering glare. "I'm mad."

"Join the club," he mutters, his eyes looking past me.

I don't care. I don't care. I don't care.

"Why are *you* mad?" I demand.

Jesus. Apparently, I *do* care.

He stops in front of Mateo's door to turn toward me. In the narrow hallway, his giant frame feels too big and too close. I am forced to inhale his delicious scent. "I'm mad about a lot of things." His voice is low and husky. "I don't have the time to tell you, and you don't have the patience or care to listen."

I open my mouth to object that maybe if he'd stop being a dick for three seconds, I might care. Before the words come out, he lifts a hand and presses a thumb to my parted lips.

"You're just a tool," he murmurs.

My brows furl together as I consider his words. *You're just a tool.* A flare of emotions glimmer in his steely blue eyes. *You're just a tool.* The intensity rippling from him indicates all this is more than just a way to climb the rungs of his career ladder. Something bubbles below the surface. Something more. A reason. A reason that eats him alive. His thumb strokes my bottom lip tenderly, and I let my guard down. I'm just a tool. Which means he's using me to get to someone else.

Mateo.

"You're using me to get to him," I say suddenly, shocked at the realization.

His gaze hardens, and he steps away from me, his nostrils flaring. "You know nothing, Poppy."

"Whatever he did to upset you, he didn't mean it. He's a good guy." I tilt my head and narrow my eyes to scrutinize him. He's breathing heavily as fury radiates from him. I've never seen him like this. "Is it about Four Fathers Freight? Is it about your brother's shares in the company?"

At my words, he visibly relaxes and barks out a harsh laugh. "Mateo is like an uncle to me."

"And yet you want to hurt him."

"Collateral damage," he bites out.

I start to tell him he's an asshole, yet again, when I hear something that makes my heart stutter in my chest.

Laughter. Feminine and happy. From Mateo's unit.

"Must be his daughter," I whisper.

"Elma is about to have another baby. She can't travel. We're Facebook friends," Camden says. "It's not his daughter."

His words have me fumbling for my key. I nearly drop my purse as I yank the key out and shove it in the door. My mind is jumbled as it tries to make sense of why Mateo's been ignoring me and why I hear a female in his home. I push through the door and see evidence of a woman. A purse and bag. Some sandals left by the door. A trail of items discarded here and there in the perfect condo Mateo obsesses over.

"Wow," Camden mutters, pointing to the couch as he closes the door behind him.

I follow his attention to the where a toddler sleeps with a blue blanket covering him. Toys are strewn all over the living room. This doesn't make sense. It's as though I've walked into the wrong condo. When I hear the laughter again, I rush toward his bedroom. There has to be an explanation. I twist the knob and push inside.

My mouth drops open in shock to see Mateo making wild love to some pretty little brunette. He has her pinned and is nipping at her neck, making her giggle each time. So playful and sweet.

So. Not. Mateo.

Mateo is a robot in the sack. He does everything with precision, gets me off easily, and when it's done, we clean up and move on to something else. There's never so much...passion.

"Who the fuck are you?" the girl yells.

"Shit!" Mateo hisses.

Strong arms grab me and pull me from the room. Camden. He closes the door behind us and walks me into Mateo's kitchen. I'm so stunned, I'm speechless. I don't even realize I'm crying until Camden cradles my face with his palms and swipes tears away with his thumbs.

"That's why he didn't call," I whisper, my chest feeling tight with the embarrassment and hurt burning through me. I squeeze my eyes shut. "That's why he didn't care."

Camden pulls me to his chest, hugging me. He's an awful human being, but in this moment, I cling to him as a sob hangs in my throat, begging for release. I can hear Mateo and the girl arguing in the room.

"I'm sure Mateo has a good explanation for this," he murmurs, kissing my hair.

I don't move or nod. I cry silently as the severity of what I just saw crashes into me. My fiancé was having an affair with someone who has a kid. The media will have fun running this story.

"Poppy," Mateo says, entering the kitchen behind

us. "Let me explain."

I flinch at his words, and Camden strokes his fingertips down my spine. His touch calms me. He may be a bastard, but at the moment, he's not the biggest bastard in the room.

"Rita and I—"

"Rita and I?" Jerking away from Camden, I turn to face Mateo. Anger surges through me. "You're a fucking couple now? What about us?"

He frowns, shame in his eyes. "There's a lot to discuss."

"So fucking discuss it!" I scream.

His face reddens, and he looks over his shoulder. "Calm down and keep quiet. You'll wake Kai up." When he turns to regard me, disappointment screws up his features. Disappointment at me for being loud when I just caught him driving into some girl.

"Too late," the girl says, entering the kitchen with the toddler on her hip.

Quickly, I size her up. Her supple lips are still swollen from kissing and her neck is red from Mateo's scruff. She blurs before me as tears continue to well in my eyes. Hastily, I swipe them away and glower at her.

"What are you? Sixteen?" I hiss.

The little boy sucks on his thumb and frowns at my tone.

"Rita is—was—my daughter's best friend." Mateo groans and scrubs at his face with one hand. "Back before you and me...when I sent my daughter off to get away from the wrong crowds, Rita and I started a thing."

Rita smirks at me.

Camden must sense my urge to claw her eyeballs out because he puts a steadying palm on my shoulder.

Mateo continues with a huff. "We fucked around, and I broke it off when things got too serious. But last week, she reached out to me. After all this time, she realized a boy needs his father and came back last week to tell me." He reaches over and fluffs the boy's hair. "When you didn't show up last night, and they did, we had a long talk. I got to know them. Reconnect with Rita. It felt right."

No.

The boy looks at me with the same innocent expression Mateo has sometimes.

Mateo is far from innocent, though.

"He's your son," I whisper.

Camden squeezes my shoulder.

"He's my son," Mateo agrees. "And..." he looks over at Rita and smiles, breaking my heart, "and we want to try to make it work. As a family."

I jerk from Camden's grasp and charge over to Mateo. With all the power I have in me, I shove him.

He barely moves. Tears roll down my cheeks as I yank the ring from my finger. I grab his wrist and deposit the diamond into his palm.

"You're going to need this then," I choke out.

I start to pull away, but he grabs my wrist, stopping me. His eyes are kind as he regards me. "We'll keep it silent. This won't affect your campaign," he vows. "Rita and I have decided we'll do whatever it takes to keep this from hurting you."

Rita and I.

"Too late," I mutter. "Too fucking late."

When I charge past him, my surprisingly supportive shadow follows after me.

NINE

CAMDEN

Six days later...

WHEN MATEO WAS CAUGHT CHEATING ON Poppy, I'd expected the tears and woe is me routine to continue out the door. But I should have known better. Poppy is fierce and strong. She cried silent tears all the way back to her house. I'd tried to go in, but she firmly told me no. I wanted to ignore her and push through anyway, but with this unexpected news with Mateo, I was worried our deal would get trashed. I needed time to think and make sure she wouldn't fuck up my meetings with the judge, police commissioner, and senator.

I look up from my laptop and watch her as she taps away on her computer in her office. No tears this week. Whatever sadness she had, she must have cried it all out Saturday. Almost a week later, and she's hardened into a viper that reminds me too much of the people I hate. I much prefer her ragged, rattled, and ruined. Right now, she's poised, focused, and angry.

"Tick tock," I say, my first indicator since Mateo broke up with her that I'm still going forward with my plan to blackmail her.

Her fingers pause on the keyboard, and her blue eyes dart to mine. "Or what? You'll fuck me?" She flashes me an icy smile. "Nobody cares if you fuck me, Camden. These little boy games you're playing are childish."

A flash of fury ignites within me. "I'm not a little boy."

She smirks. "I allowed you to keep your meetings since your career is so important to you, but I will not be blackmailed into forcing my father to meet with you. You have nothing to hold over me. Everyone knows I'm no longer engaged to Mateo."

I lift a brow. "How do you figure?"

She taps her knuckle on her screen. "This."

I rise from my chair and walk around the desk until I'm behind her. Placing my hands on the top of her leather chair, I lean in to read an article in the *Tampa Times*.

Tampa's Golden Girl Tarnished

I grit my teeth as I skim the article. It's all bullshit she fed to a reporter. Mostly, it's a watered-down version of the actual events. Her fiancé found out about a son he had and wanted to make it work with the mother and their child. Poppy and Mateo parted as friends and wish each other the best.

Cue fucking eye roll.

"So, there. You have nothing on me," she snaps. "And after today, you can find someone else to intern for because it sure as hell won't be me."

I pull her chair away from the desk and roughly spin her toward me. She lets out a squeak of surprise. I grab the arms of her chair, pinning her wrists, and glower down at her.

"It's not that fucking easy," I growl, lowering my face until we're inches apart. "I think you seem to have forgotten about our past."

"We have no past," she spits out.

"Not one you want to tell anyone," I utter, an evil grin turning my lips up. "What about the time we made out when I was fifteen?"

"You're such a liar!" she yells at me. "No one will believe you because it didn't happen!"

"Money can buy you anything," I tell her coldly. "It can buy me witnesses. It can buy me someone to forge motherfucking love letters and date them years ago. It can buy me photoshopped pictures of whatever the hell I want."

"You wouldn't."

"You know I will. I can have whatever I want inside of an hour. Test me, Poppy. Fucking test me. All you had to do was get me one more goddamn meeting. Why are you being so difficult? I swore I'd be out of your hair the moment you got me that meeting."

Her hard gaze weakens. "Why do you want it so bad? Why is it so important?"

"It just is," I mutter.

The other three went off exactly as I planned. Those men know exactly where they stand in my world and it's below my fucking feet. They've promised me the entire goddamn world, and for now, I'll zip my lips.

Until I get my last meeting.

Then, I'm going to make a mess of everything.

"Call him."

"I've tried every day this week," she says, pouting.

"Try again."

"No."

I arch a brow. "You have to."

"I'm not calling him again, so do what you must. I'll try again next week."

"Then that means you failed," I murmur, my gaze skimming down to her lips. "That means I'm going to fuck you."

"My failure doesn't guarantee your success," she challenges, licking her lips. The action has my cock wide fucking awake. "I wonder if you'll have to drug me again. I'm wondering if you're compensating for something. I mean, who has to drug a woman—"

I grip her wrist and haul her hand to my cock straining in my slacks. "I can assure you, I can back up my big ego with my even bigger dick."

She gapes at me. "You're awfully confident."

"You creamed your panties the first time I flirted with you," I tell her smugly, using her hand to stroke me through my clothes. Her fingers are stiff at first, but then she relaxes them. "Your pretty face turned pink any time I looked at you. You wanted me to fuck you. You went home and fingered your perfect cunt to thoughts of me deep inside."

"Camden..."

"I'm going to spend days showing you just how much your body wants me, Poppy. Days."

I pull away and start packing my shit up.

"W-What? Now? No. I have crap to do and—"

"Nope. I cleared your calendar."

"But I can't leave in the middle of the—"

"You're going."

"I have all this work that needs—"

I unplug her laptop and snap it closed. She grumbles when I shove it in her messenger bag. "Let's roll, Popps. We're losing daylight."

"It's not even noon. We're not losing daylight," she huffs, but starts gathering her things.

She's going a little too easily...

I swivel around as she shoulders her purse and storm over to her. My hand grips her throat, and I press a kiss to her lips. When she gasps in surprise, I plunge my tongue into her mouth. I kiss her in a threatening way.

A way that says I'm smarter. More powerful. And richer. So don't try to play me.

Whatever fucked up game she thinks she can play to screw me over is pointless.

I will win.

When I pull away, her eyes are closed and her cheeks are pink. The tough woman from earlier is gone and this soft, almost smiling one is in her place. Confusion wars within me.

This was supposed to be difficult.

Yet, here she is, looking all too eager to fuck her intern.

"Let's go," I bark as I gather my stuff and stalk over to her door. I open it and usher her out. Nellie shoots me a pitiful fucking stare, but I ignore her. All week, she's tried talking to me, but I've given her the cold shoulder.

Only one woman has my attention.

"We'll be out for the rest of the afternoon. Meetings," I lie as we pass Nellie.

She nods, but I can tell she doesn't believe me. I flash her one of my smoldering grins and wink at her. All animosity bleeds from her as she blushes. "See you Monday."

Poppy remains quiet until we're in my car cruising down the road. "Where are we going?" she asks finally. "Your place or mine?"

I snort. "Neither."

"The hotel?"

"Nope."

She lets out a huff of frustration, but I ignore her. I turn on some music and stew over the fact that I'm not getting that meeting with the mayor. I'll get it one way or another. For now, I'll take fucking joy in defiling his heartbroken daughter. That'll make up for one loss by giving me a win I am all too happy to claim.

I glance over at Poppy and she's stiff. Tense and ready for a fight. She really thinks she'll be able to pull some shit when I get her naked. That she won't enjoy it or be able to shame me for my lack of play in the bedroom. She has no idea what I'm capable of. Whatever she and Mateo did was nothing compared to how I'm going to disrupt her world.

Breaking her will be fun.

Definitely a win.

We pull up to Kipper's Marina and I park in my

assigned spot. I love the confusion that radiates from her, but she refuses to give voice to.

"Let's go," I grumble.

"Why are we here?" she asks as she reaches for her messenger bag.

"Leave it," I instruct. "You'll have everything you need on the boat."

"Boat?"

My Azimut S7 is my newest baby. Grandad bought me my first diecast yacht when I was a little kid and I've been obsessed ever since. Now, instead of collecting metal boats or making them from model kits, I just buy them.

God, I love money.

Sometimes, I wonder if I'm more like my father than I'd like to admit. I used to marvel at how he could buy anything he wanted whenever he wanted. Once, I asked him for a Ulysse Nardin Tourbillon watch. I was fourteen. All it took was a big smile and telling him he was a good dad. Ten minutes later, he was on the phone with a rep putting in a custom order for a two-hundred-thousand-dollar watch. I was proud as fuck of that watch too. Wore it every day until my dad died. Now, it sits in a drawer. Hidden away. Just like the rest of my memories of him.

"You don't have to run!" Poppy calls out from

behind me.

I slow, realizing I was hoofing it along. Memories of my father are conflicting. Everyone wants someone to blame. It was his parties. His friends. His world. All of what was exposed to me nearly ruined me. But deep down in my bitter heart, I know it's not completely true. It's just not something I want to think about right now. Right now, I have other shit to focus on. Reflecting back on how my dad wasn't as awful as my brothers claim is a Band-Aid that can be pulled off another day.

When I hit the dock and the warm sea air blows on my face, the tension bleeds from me. Poppy's heels clack on the wood behind me. I'm not sure I'll be able to relax with her in my space, but I have no choice. She's here, and I'm ready to make her pay. I'll fuck her and send her on her way. After that, I can come back and plot some more.

Always plotting.

"Poppy," I say, motioning to my Azimut. "Meet *Lady Vindicta*. She's sleek like a panther. Fancy as fuck too. But when I get my hands on her and get her out on the water, she purrs like a little kitten."

Her brows lift, but I can see a gleam of excitement in her crystal blue eyes that match the cloudless sky. "Yours is the only black boat out here. It's pretty."

"Custom paint job. They call it soulless abyss."

She purses her lips, as if remembering why she's here, and steps onto my boat.

No getting away now, Poppy.

TEN

POPPY

HE BELONGS HERE. PREPPY AS HELL AND ARROGANT. Camden Pearson grew up with a silver spoon in his mouth and wouldn't know real life if it popped him upside the head. Spoiled rotten. He has that awful father of his to thank for that. Eric was a dick of epic proportions. It's no wonder he spawned little hellions.

Camden is most definitely born from the depths of hell.

Soulless abyss.

How fitting is that paint color?

All irritated thoughts of Camden and his father drain away as I step onto the most beautiful boat I've ever seen. Dad has a pontoon boat, but it's laughable in comparison.

"Shoes off when you go below deck," Camden grunts from behind me.

I stop to pull off my heels and hold them in my hand as I watch him effortlessly untie his yacht from the dock. He motions to a door that leads to the cabin.

"If you look in the middle drawer by the closet, my brother Nixon's wife left her swimsuit last time they used *Lady Vindicta*. Go put it on," he instructs as he moves to sit in the captain's chair. "Now, Poppy."

I flip him the bird, ignoring the way his deep chuckle sends shivers down my spine, and walk down the steep stairs to the cabin. I'm shocked at how spacious it is. Everything is clean and sleek. White walls. White, faux fur blanket on the bed. Bright lights and the scent of oranges. Perfection. My feet on the soft, plush, pale gray carpet has me sighing. I toss my shoes in the corner, along with my purse. For once, I don't miss my laptop. The boat starts moving, but it's smooth and the rumble of the engine is quiet. I know he's here to punish me and show me what a little badass he is, but I'm secretly thrilled to take a break from the stressful week I've had.

Mateo.

Annoyance flitters through me.

Saturday, I'd been embarrassed. That was why I cried. Knowing some young thing shows up and he practically forgets my name hurt. Sure, they had a history before me, but it still stung.

Stung but didn't destroy.

It's times like these I wish my mother were still alive. She took her life a decade ago. It was a rocky time for me. Dad, like always, hardened his heart and acted as though it didn't bother him. I always resented him for that. For once in his life, I wanted him soft—soft when it mattered. Dad doesn't know how to be soft, though. He kept on while I spun in circles, lost.

I open the first drawer, and my flesh heats when I see an array of vibrators, handcuffs, and other kinky things, though I have no idea what they are. Unease flitters through me as I consider Camden using them on me.

Unease.

Not excitement.

My heart stutters.

I can't even lie to myself. Pathetic.

Huffing, I slam the drawer shut and open the second one. There are a couple swimsuits. Both skimpy. One is black, and the other is white. If he's going to play devil, then I'll play angel. I pull out the white one and quickly change into it. The triangles barely cover my nipples, much less the globes of my breasts. It's a tiny scrap of nothing, but one quick glance in the full-length mirror tells me I look hot. If I'm going to dance with the devil, I may as well look good doing it. After throwing my hair in a messy bun and grabbing my sunglasses, I climb up the stairs and find Camden.

He's shed his suit jacket and tie. His sleeves are now

rolled up his toned, tanned forearms, and his Aviators are perched on his nose. They're mirrored, so I can only see my reflection rather than his piercing blue eyes. I try not to focus on how much the little suit reveals. Instead, I walk up to him and motion to the steering wheel.

"I didn't know you knew much about boats." I cross my arms over my chest, worrying about my appearance.

"A lot you don't know about me," he rumbles, the sound sexy and enticing.

I shiver and avoid his hidden stare to look out at the ocean. The waters are calm, and we practically glide across. When he guns the engine, I lose my footing and stumble into him. His strong arm hooks around my waist and he pulls me into his lap. My barely-covered ass rubs against his obvious erection. The thought that I turn him on turns *me* on.

Fuck, I am in deep shit with him.

His palm splays over my stomach, and my breath hitches as I realize just how big his hand is. I try to focus on the sparkly water, but it's difficult when his thumb rubs me just below my breast.

"Have you ever driven a boat?" he asks, his hot breath tickling my shoulder.

"I drove my dad's pontoon boat a few times."

He grunts as though he's not pleased by my

answer. "The pontoon is like a minivan. *Lady Vindicta* is like the Bugatti." His left hand grips mine, while his right stays planted on my stomach. "Put your hand here," he instructs, his voice husky. "I need you to drive."

"Why?"

"Because my hands will be busy."

Heat pools in my core, and I try not to rub against his cock. The fact that my body turns on this young hottie has some of my self-esteem returning. After my humiliating breakup, I'm still a little fragile. My ego took a beating, and it's nice to feel wanted again.

"What will your hands be doing?" I ask, my words breathy and too needy.

His left hand grips my thigh and squeezes. "Exploring." He slides his palm up my leg until his thumb meets the fabric of my swimsuit bottoms. "Keep your eyes ahead."

I bite on my lip and stare out at the water. I don't see anything, but he has me on edge.

"White's an interesting color," he observes. "Screams innocence."

"Seems fitting," I argue.

His teeth bite into my shoulder, but not hard enough to hurt too bad. Then his tongue runs along the new grooves in my flesh, soothing the indentions. "Your screams will be far from innocent."

Before I can come up with a haughty remark, his fingers slide along the edge of my bottoms, barely sliding beneath them. My heart races and my skin flushes with heat. When he pulls his hand away to rub my thigh again, I groan in irritation.

"What?" he taunts. "Does the babysitter like it when she gets touched here?" His fingers dip below the edge once more.

"Don't be weird," I grumble.

He laughs, and it sounds genuine. "I'm not the one getting naked on a yacht with a man she hates." His fingers tug slightly at the strings on one side of swimsuit bottoms. The bow falls loose and the material starts to slide away. His palm leaves my stomach and he does the same with the other side. My heart stammers in my chest. I should stop this or put up a fight. What I shouldn't do is lean my back against his chest.

"You want this," he breathes against my neck. "Who knows for how long you've wanted this..."

I groan at another one of his stupid insinuations. Camden Pearson wasn't even a thought until he showed up in Mateo's kitchen two weeks ago looking hot and smug and irresistible. "I don't want this."

He laughs again.

I don't even get mad because it's a lie.

I'm afraid of how much I want this.

Whatever *this* is.

He wants to ruin me for some reason, and I'm letting him—willingly. My father would be horrified at my behavior. Then again, had he not blown me off, I wouldn't be in this position to begin with.

"Are you drugged?" he asks before biting my neck.

"N-No."

"Am I forcing you?"

His fingers nudge the fabric. All it would take is a flick of his fingers and it would fall away, leaving me bare to him.

"Stop teasing me," I breathe.

"This would be teasing," he counters as his longest finger inches lower, until it slips between my lower lips and whispers over my clit. I let out a needy moan in response. When he pulls his hand back up, I growl.

"Stop."

"Stop touching you?"

"Stop teasing me, asshole. Do whatever you're going to do and let's get this over with."

He pushes away the bottoms and runs his finger down my slit again. I shudder in his arms, my eyes slamming shut. Quickly, I pop them back open.

"Stop the boat," I beg. "I...I can't focus."

His chuckles are like gasoline to the flames flickering inside me. Lust has become an inferno, obliterating all common sense. I've barely registered he's turned off the boat and we're just coasting.

"You haven't even gone swimming yet and you're probably already soaked," he observes.

"Don't flatter yourself," I lie.

His finger pushes against my very much wet and ready opening. A groan rasps from me as he easily slides inside. His lips press tender kisses between not-so-tender bites on my shoulder. The beast that lives within him seems to war with the gentleman he's groomed himself to be. I'm fascinated to witness him as both a cruel-tongued monster and the master who plays my body like an instrument.

"Feel this?" he breathes against my skin as he presses in deep and curls his finger. Pleasure pulsates from my core, making my eyes flutter closed and my head fall back.

"Yessss."

"That spot is where I will own you, Poppy." He rubs me there again, sending more shockwaves through me. "Do you agree?"

"Yes," I mutter, no longer caring to keep up pretenses. Right now, he's giving me something I've never felt before. I've come tons of times, but it's all been from my clit—not my g-spot. Such an elusive and silly notion. The few boyfriends I've had over the years never found it. I certainly never had. Camden acts like he's known exactly where it was all along.

"You're so fucking juicy," he growls. "My finger is soaked because of you, dirty girl. I thought you hated me. Yet here you are drenching me. I think you lie to me, but mostly, you lie to yourself."

His taunts only serve to turn me on more. I find my thighs clenching and quivering with need. In the afternoon heat, I feel too hot and sweaty.

"Do you want to come?" he asks, nipping at my neck.

"Yes."

"Beg me."

"Ugh," I complain.

He rubs me in a delicious way. Maybe if I ignore him...

His finger starts sliding out, and I panic. "Please. I want it. It feels good," I admit with a huff. "Don't stop."

"Much better." As he rubs me inside, he ignores my clit altogether. It makes me want him to touch me there too. I imagine his tongue there, which only serves to make me wetter. When his other palm cups my breast, I clench around his finger. "Don't worry. I can't ignore these perfect tits for long, baby."

Baby.

The sentiment is so simple and so sweet, and

it foolishly has me warming to him. He's so cool and composed. The ragged way he said "baby" just unravels me. I'm spinning, mixed up with confusing thoughts and glorious touch, when he pulls my top to the side. His fingers touch my bare flesh, and he gently pinches my hardened nipple.

"These nipples are perfect for biting," he tells me, tugging hard enough that I cry out. The zing of pain sends pulses of pleasure rippling from my core. "And you want to get bitten."

Do I?

My past lovers never bit me.

But the idea of being sprawled beneath Camden as he bruises my flesh dizzies me.

"You think you know everything," I murmur.

"I know you better than you think." He pulls on my nipple again. "Your cunt squeezes when I do that." Then he bites my shoulder. "And when I do that."

He continues to abuse my nipple as he bites at my neck until I become overwhelmed with pleasure. With one finger inside me, two pinching me, and a mouthful of teeth sinking into my throat, I come like a wild heathen. A loud, brazen scream, and I let go. My vision becomes a blast of bright white as every nerve ending starting from my core explodes through me. I shudder in his grip and nearly slide to the floor as I lose myself to an orgasm.

The best orgasm I've ever had.

Shame threatens to make me feel bad, but then I remember I'm single. Single women can come all they want and enjoy it. They don't even have to feel guilty. He may be the enemy, but he played my body like we were on the same team.

His finger slides out of me and he pops my pussy hard enough to make my cry out.

"I'm hungry. Let's cook lunch."

ELEVEN

C A M D E N

'M AMUSED THAT SHE'S BEEN POUTING SINCE lunch. Since I gave her an earthshattering orgasm and then forced her to calm down so we could eat. She glowered as I ordered her to cut vegetables. Frowned as we ate the filets I cooked in the skillet. Looked fucking miserable as I chatted about current events and her campaign.

Now, she's lying on the top of the boat, soaking up the sun and ignoring me. Torturing her is what makes my dick hard. While she acts like a bratty teenager, I change into my swim trunks in the cabin and attempt to settle my cock. That was the real reason I stopped what we were doing from going any further. I was three seconds from impaling her on my dick. But that would mean losing control.

I don't lose control.

I'm going to tease and taunt her. Draw this shit out until she's begging for me. By the time I get off this boat, she'll be creaming her panties any time she looks my way. I smirk as I go above deck.

"Are you going to pout all day?" I sneer.

"Fuck you."

"You certainly wish."

She scrambles to her feet and glowers at me. Her chest heaves with fury. "No. What I wish is for you to take me home."

"Not going to happen."

"Your mind games are better suited for some dumb college girl," she hisses.

"You like it when I mind fuck you, baby. You wish I'd fuck your pussy too."

She storms forward and shoves me, catching me off guard. I stumble back a few steps, then charge her way. With her plump lips parted and sexy as fuck, the urge to kiss her is overwhelming. As I prowl toward her, she slips.

It happens so fast.

Fumble. Thud. Splash.

The moment she falls and knocks her head on the side of the boat before flipping off the edge, I'm already moving. When I reach the side, her body sinks under the surface. I don't hesitate before diving in after her. With my eyes open, ignoring the burn of the ocean, I swim hard toward her. Four years as a varsity swimmer in high school and now in my first year of college, I have faith in my abilities when out in the ocean. I've just never tried to save anyone before.

Her blonde hair has come free of her bun and I swipe out, grabbing a handful. I'm able to draw her to me and then kick powerfully toward the surface. As soon as I reach air, I gasp a lungful of it, then swim us over to the back of the boat where the ladder is. She doesn't make a sound, which has terror rising up in me.

"Poppy," I bark out as I climb into the boat with her. "Poppy!"

I lay her on her back and stare down at her bluish face. It scares the fuck out of me. My lifeguard training kicks in, and I begin performing CPR. Thank God it only takes a second before she's sputtering and coughing up salty ocean water. Once she realizes where she's at and what's happened, fat crocodile tears well in her eyes. Her bottom lip trembles, and fuck if I don't forget every angry thought I have against her.

"Shhh," I murmur as I haul her into my lap and wrap my arms around her. "You're okay. I wasn't going to let anything happen to you."

She sobs and clings to me. I stroke my fingers along her wet skin while kissing the top of her head. I hold her for hours, the sun warming us until it begins to set on the horizon.

"Popps," I grunt. "Wake up."

"I'm tired," she complains.

"And if you hurt your head, the last thing you should do is nap. Stay awake and talk to me," I say softly.

When she ignores me to snuggle closer, I stand with her in my arms. I carry her down into the cabin and set her to her feet in front of the shower.

"Take a warm shower. You'll feel better. I'll make us something to eat for dinner." I start the shower and open the door for her.

"Camden..." she chokes out. "I'm sorry."

"For falling off the boat?"

Her nose turns pink. "For whatever hurt you."

Anger surges up inside me, reminding me of my purpose. I start tugging at the strings of her swimsuit until she's naked, then grab her biceps and walk her into the shower.

"Stop talking," I snap.

She grips my shoulders before I can back away. "No."

"Shower. Now."

In a bold move, she flings her body against mine. Her bare tits pressed against my chest has my fury transforming into something more passionate. My cock lurches in my trunks, eager to get to her. As though she's inside my head, her hand slides between us to push down my trunks. When my aching dick is in her tiny hand, I groan out in pleasure.

"Fuck," I complain. "Fuck."

This was not how it was supposed to go down. Yet here I am, fusing my lips to hers and pushing her into the tiny ass shower. I let my trunks fall to my feet and step out of them. My hands grip her fleshy ass and lift her.

"I'm not using a condom," I threaten.

"I'm on the pill."

"You're not afraid?" I ask as I rub my dick against her slick opening.

"You dove into the ocean to save me from drowning. I doubt you'd willingly hurt me." She kisses me hard before pulling away to look at me with the softest, sweetest stare. "I trust you."

Dumb girl.

Dumb fucking girl.

You don't trust a monster.

I line the crown of my dick against her wet heat and drive hard inside her. She screams and claws at my shoulders, but I don't give her any chance to escape. I grip her ass, lean her against the wall, and fuck the fire out of her. Her lips and teeth are desperate as they attempt to touch me everywhere. We're both lost to the moment. No longer enemies. Just two needy souls. A black, twisted one, and this sweeter one bred from a villain.

"Camden," she cries out. "Oh God."

I kiss her deep and grind into her, rubbing her clit in just the right way. When her nails dig in deeper and she screams in ecstasy, I lose control. My cock throbs as I come deep inside her, filling her the fuck up with my pleasure. An animalistic possessive growl resounds from me.

I've lost my goddamn mind.

Abruptly, I pull her off my dick and rinse off while she holds herself, watching me warily.

"Make it quick," I bark out and leave her.

I need to get a hold of myself before I do something stupid.

Like claim her for good.

———

"Smells good," she says softly as she enters the dining area.

My eyes, eager to drink her in, skim over her appearance. All the makeup on her face is gone, making her look more my age, and her blonde hair is down in wet, messy waves. She's stolen one of my t-shirts and more of that male pride surges inside me. I like the way the white fabric reveals her peaked nipples. She's naked under the shirt. And I fucking love that.

"Sit," I grunt.

I've set up her place across the table from me.

But as soon as I take my seat, she picks up her plate and glass to move closer. I try to ignore her as we eat, but she happily chirps about how good the food is.

"I didn't know you could cook." Her leg brushes against mine, and I move it away.

"Nobody does."

She sips her tea and frowns at me. "Why not?"

I shrug. "My brothers like to feel like they're taking care of me. I let them."

"So you hold out on them? What an injustice." She inhales her food, then curls up next to me, leaning against me. I don't push her away despite wanting to. "Do you live on this boat? Mateo always told me you lived with Hayden. I snooped around after my shower. You have like five thousand watches."

"Nosey," I say, leaning back in my seat.

She tilts her head up to look at me. Her blue eyes are clear and curious. I fucked her and was an ass to her, yet she's still here snooping, literally and figuratively. I'm not sure I'll ever be ready to lift some of the lids in my mind.

Especially not by her.

"I live with my brother, but he's proposing to his girl, Katie. I'll be looking for a place now. Somewhere near the beach."

"Does Trevor Blackstone still own all that

property? Maybe he could sell you something. I know your family is close to him." She goes quiet for a moment. "I'm sorry about your parents."

Emotion aches in my chest, and I hate it.

I tear my gaze from hers to think about my father.

———

"Go play," he grunts, motioning with his head outside.

His friends smirk my way. Some unknowing. Others watch me like I'm a little steak on Dad's grill they want to eat. I don't like them. Especially him.

Gladly, I start for the door when I hear his voice.

"Your father says you're into boats now?" the one I hate the most says to me.

"He's got an entire collection," Dad says.

One of his friends moves to sit closer to him, telling him about a freight company in Hong Kong. The one I hate most rises from his seat.

"I'd love to see it, little boy."

I cringe. I hate when he calls me "little boy." I'm eleven now. I'm not little.

I want Mateo or Uncle Trevor or Dad to notice how much I hate this guy, but they don't. They've joined the conversation, all talking animatedly about the subject. The one I hate grips my shoulder and guides me from the room. He takes me to my bedroom, but the lock is worthless now because we've walked right in. Together. I stand in the middle of the room, frozen in fear as he picks up each and every model boat I have. When he's done, he turns his scary look my way.

Big smile.

Handsome.

I know because the women throw themselves at him now that his wife is dead. I wish they'd keep him away from me.

"I want to show you something in the bathroom, little boy."

Black. Black. Black.

My mind erases horrors I will never think of again. Pain assaults me in places it shouldn't. I want to throw up. I want to cry. But I'm still frozen.

"Remember what we talked about?" he asks, petting my hair like he's some good, kind uncle.

I swallow and stare at the floor.

"Tell me."

"I'm gross and my dad will be embarrassed of me."

"And?"

"If anyone finds out, they'll take me away from my brothers. They don't let gross boys stay with their brothers."

"And?"

"Your best friend is the boss of all the policemen. He'll put me in jail too."

"Do you believe it?"

I lift my gaze, chancing a look at him. His stare is hard, and he isn't smiling at me. "Yes."

"Good boy."

———

The past weighs me down, shackling me. I feel like a prisoner to it some days and the memories are my sentence. Hate, deep and unending, festers inside me. It's a beast that cannot be killed. I don't want to kill it. I want to free it and let it feed on that motherfucker. So often, I'm good at compartmentalizing and controlling where my brain goes. But with Poppy, it's like my emotions are running rampant—both good and bad. I'm suffocating with all the air around me, free for the taking.

My lungs are clamped tight, refusing to suck in the air. Fuck, maybe it's a panic attack. Whatever it is, when I get like this, I like to swim. The water frees my mind—frees my goddamn soul. Since I can't breathe anyway, I can glide through the waters and calm my shuttering heart.

Poppy must sense the change within me. She's desperately attempting to hold on to me—figuratively and mentally. There's no holding me back when I'm escaping him, though. I'm faster and smarter. Always two steps ahead. I tear from her grasp and leave her calling after me.

"Camden!"

I charge out of the too small cabin with the memories chasing my ass like fire on a gasoline trail.

Once I'm above deck, I run over to the edge and dive into the dark waters. Now that it's dark out, it's like the water can suck you down and never let go.

Sometimes I want that.

I want to forget.

I want to burn away every horrible memory of my past.

Deep, deep, deep, I swim until the water becomes chilly and my chest burns with the need for air. Sucking in all the water and letting the current take me away is all it would take. The bad shit would drown with me. Losing my mom to our psychotic neighbor. My dad's murder. The man I hate hurting me. My brother Hayden nearly losing his life.

And her.

Images of her head tilted back in pleasure as I fucked her in the small shower have me kicking. Memories of her plump lips pressed to mine have me swimming hard to the surface. *Goddamn you, Poppy Beckett. I'm supposed to be using you in this game of revenge, but the things I want to do to you are far too sweet to be called such an ugly word.*

I break the surface and inhale a big gasp of air. Finally, I can breathe. Those memories don't own my lungs and my heart. I'm stronger than them. The yacht bobs on the surface, the lights glowing on the water. A shadow paces along the deck and calls out for me. Then, I hear a splash. I swim over to where she's jumped in. She treads water, the t-shirt glued to her. Once I reach her, I pull her to me.

"I'm sorry," she chokes out, her eyes glassy in the moonlight. She's almost weightless as she wraps her body around mine. I easily swim in place, keeping us both afloat. Her fingers brush back my hair and she kisses my mouth. The way she kisses me is sad but insistent. As though her kiss has the power to fucking heal me. When her tongue seeks out mine, my mind gets lost to her. Maybe she does have some kind of power. I'm no longer thinking about the bad stuff. I'm thinking about how I want to fuck her right here in the water.

"Come on," I mutter against her mouth as I swim us over to the ladder. "Hold on."

She grips the ladder with her back against the rungs but keeps her legs wrapped around me. I fumble with my trunks, then push my cock against her pussy. We both groan as I easily slide in. I grip her ass with one hand and hold onto the ladder with the other as I fuck her right here in the ocean. She greedily kisses me, and I let her nip at my lips and suck on my tongue. I let her devour me while I thrust into her wildly. We're both breathing heavily and moaning.

"Touch your clit," I order, my voice husky and

filled with need. I hate for her to see me weak like this. So fucking desperate.

"We fit so good together," she moans as her fingers rub on her clit and her cunt clenches.

"Don't get used to it," I snap, but the usual venom is missing.

She grins, looking all too fucking pretty. "Too late, Camden. I'm already addicted. I want to turn all the calendar days pink."

Something about her words has me relaxing and forgetting, just for a moment, that she's part of a bigger scheme. I fuck this girl because she's hot and intelligent and funny. I fuck her because I had a crush on her when I was a kid and an obsession with her as an adult. I fuck her because she's mine.

"Yesss," she whimpers, her body seizing in pleasure.

It pushes me over the edge, and I let out a garbled sound. My nuts tighten, and then I'm spilling my seed into her. I've been with a lot of girls, but I always wrap my dick up. I don't want any accidental pregnancies or a fucking disease. With Poppy, it's like I can't even bear anything between us. I want to fill her up with my cum and watch it run down her legs.

"I've never been fucked in the ocean," she says dreamily. "I think this is the best sex I've ever had."

"Think?" I taunt.

Her laughter is musical and sweet. "Fine, arrogant ass. It was the best sex second to that shower romp earlier."

Because I'm a dick, I press her buttons. "Better than Mateo?"

Her brows scrunch together, and I instantly regret my words. "Mateo was very calculated. It went exactly the same way each time." She looks away. "He got me off, it was just that..." she trails off. "Nothing."

I arch a brow at her. "Don't lie, Poppy. You're awful at it."

Her gaze meets mine again. "He didn't like to cuddle." She bites on her lip and her nostrils flare. "God, I am pathetic. No wonder he fucked some young girl the moment she bounced along."

I bite her chin, and then her neck, and then her earlobe. "He was an idiot."

"Why do you want to hurt me, Camden?" she asks, her voice shaky and unsure. "I feel like we could be so good together."

I close my eyes and bring forth all the reasons why. The normal burning hate is a dull throb tonight.

"I don't specifically want to hurt you," I admit, pressing a kiss to her neck just below her ear. "I want to hurt *him*. You're just collateral damage."

She tenses and tries to pull away, but I suck on her neck until her clenching cunt has my dick hard inside her again. This girl, knowing I'm with her because of some fucked up reason, lets me fuck her until she screams over and over again.

Focus, Camden.

Focus on the prize.

Focus on destroying him.

TWELVE

P O P P Y

I WAKE SLIGHTLY DISORIENTED BUT WARM. A strong, naked body is wrapped around me as though I might disappear in his sleep. It makes my heart flutter in my chest. I tilt my head to look at him. His normally gelled hair is messy and all over the place, a lock fallen into his eyes. Long for a man, but super sexy, eyelashes fan over his cheeks. His mouth is parted as he sleeps, his hot breath tickling my chest.

He's beautiful.

Looks as though he's an angel when he sleeps.

I'd thought he looked like a devil. Like his father. But the more I peel back Camden's layers, I realize he's still an angel. An avenging angel. Something about me and the people I know has him all riled up. Hell, he's named his boat Lady Revenge. I didn't tell him I took Latin and remembered what Vindicta meant. It was just another piece in a complicated puzzle. It doesn't take a rocket scientist to realize it has something to do with my dad, though. He hates him. I can see it in the way his icy eyes always flash with fury. The way his jaw clenches and he fists his hands.

What did Dad do to him?

I know my dad and Camden's father had a falling out not long after my mom died. I'd walked in on the argument and worried I'd have to call the cops. My mind drifts to that day.

━━━━━━

"If I find out you did anything, I will hire every motherfucking hitman on this planet to hunt you down at the same goddamn time!" Eric Pearson roars.

I stand in the doorway to my father's office, my hand covering my mouth in horror. Eric has my dad pushed against the wall, his hands around his throat as he yells in his face. My dad's eyes are wide and his face is purple.

"Dad!" I cry out. "Eric, let him go!"

Eric's hate-filled glare snaps to mine, and I stumble as I walk toward them, fear skittering up my spine. Being a public official, I know Dad has enemies. But Eric Pearson? I thought they were friends.

"Go, Poppy. This doesn't concern you," Eric hisses at me.

I swallow down my fear and rush over to him. Reluctantly, he releases my father when I pull him away. As soon as my dad is free, I throw myself into his arms and hug him.

Eric's glare is evil and deadly. Solely for my father. "You so much as step foot near anyone in my family, you will regret it." He then glowers at me. "I will come after everything you own, Marshall. Everything." Eric licks his lips in an openly salacious way that insinuates he means me. Dad hugs me tighter.

"Understood, but whatever it is you're thinking, you're wrong," Dad huffs. I can hear the fear in his voice. Like when Mom killed herself. It scares me that he's afraid.

"I'll pry it out of him. I know you fucking did something."

"You're poorly mistaken," Dad snaps back.

Eric narrows his eyes at my father, and then he's gone.

"Oh, Dad," I cry out, hugging him tight. "He's such a dick!"

He strokes my hair and kisses my head. "He won't get my girl," he assures me.

All Dad's words sound like lies. Shaky and weak. I hope the last one for sure isn't a lie. Eric looks like he'd be the type of guy to eat a girl like me for dinner.

———

My memory fades as kisses drag me back to the present. Kisses on my breast. A tongue on my nipple. When I look down, piercing blue eyes meet mine. In this moment, they're missing their edge and hatefulness. He looks happy. Happy on Camden is beautiful. I find myself tearing up.

What happened to you?

What did my father do to you?

My father is stern, but he doesn't hurt people. Surely Eric was jumping to the wrong conclusion. Dad's friends are sleazeballs, but not Dad. Senator John Ham, on the other hand, is the worst. On more than one occasion, John has made advances on me. Not all of those advances were on this side of eighteen either. I remember clearly when I was sixteen and he slapped my ass when I walked by. All he did was wink at me, like it wasn't a big deal. I remember feeling shocked and grossed out. He was so old. Then, years later, when I was home for the holidays, he tried to kiss me. John was drunk and over for one of Dad's parties. He got his tongue down my throat before I managed to push him away.

"What are you thinking about?" Camden asks. "It's not about me. You're trembling." His intense eyes bore into mine. "Talk to me, Beckett."

With a huff, I let it out. "John Ham forced a kiss on me once. He's a pervert."

He jerks away and sits up in bed. Rage radiates from him like heat from the sun. Overpowering. Deadly. "He touched you?"

"Just a kiss," I groan, grabbing his hand. "It's fine. I'm used to stuff like that."

Fury morphs his features into something devilish for sure. "No one should ever have to be used to stuff like that."

"Don't get all sanctimonious on me now, Camden," I grumble, embarrassed at his over-the-top response. "You did worse when you drugged me, stripped me, and then tried to blackmail me with pictures of us."

The anger leeches from his features. "Poppy..."

"I'm just saying," I tell him softly.

He blinks and frowns. "I'm sorry."

I smile, because his words hit their intended mark. I feel them. "I know."

"I wasn't really going to show anyone," he admits. "I just wanted to scare you."

"You succeeded," I breathe. "Scared the hell out of me."

He presses a kiss to my lips, then starts kissing down my body. Between my breasts. Along my tan stomach. His strong hands pry my thighs apart, and then his perfect mouth is on my pussy. A low groan rumbles through me when his hot, wet tongue slides between my lips, licking all the good spots in one swipe. I jolt on the soft bed and cry out. My fingers grip his disheveled hair, and I urge him to continue. He chuckles, hot and breathy, against my most sensitive place, sending more thrills down my spine.

"I'm going to make up for that," he tells me, pressing a kiss to my clit. "I promise."

When he sucks my clit into his mouth and I lose all sense of reality, I realize he's quickly been forgiven.

"It might take a few times for me to get past it," I lie. I'm so past it. I'm nearly toppling over the edge.

"However long it takes, I'll get us there."

His words drift beyond sex and pleasure and blackmail. They needle themselves into my heart, and I feel them. Painful and exciting. I feel alive. Not just some robot on track to a career and a white picket fence.

He makes me bleed, and I like it.

But Camden Pearson is the type to keep stabbing away. I just wonder how much of his brutality I can take. My heart isn't as tough as the exterior I put up for all to see. Camden has the power not only to poke holes in my heart, but to suck every bit of happiness I have left out of me.

Let's just hope he fills me back up with something worth having in its place.

———

"You're burnt," he says as he saunters onto the deck in nothing but his swim trunks holding a bottle of water. From behind my sunglasses, I stare at his sculpted, tan chest. Beautiful golden boy. A perfect match for Tampa's Golden Girl.

"Is that for me?" My mouth waters, but from an entirely different type of thirst.

He chuckles as he hands me the bottle and sits down next to me. "You didn't have that back in your pageant days," he says, motioning to a starfish tattoo on my hip bone.

I lift a brow. "How do you know?"

He smirks. "You were this hot college chick competing in swimsuit competitions. You better believe I printed that shit out and had it under my mattress."

"Gross," I say, snorting with laughter. "You did not."

"I always knew Tampa's Golden Girl was going to be *my* girl one day..." he trails off, the lightheartedness bleeding away. His body is tense beside me.

"You've been plotting against my dad since then?" I ask, my brows furrowing in confusion. "Did he hurt you?"

I try to recall any times we were all there at the Pearson house. Camden was always laughing and playing with his brothers. I don't recall my father ever really even speaking to him.

"There's a restaurant about five miles from here. I was thinking we'd go there for lunch today," he says, ignoring my question.

"I have no clothes except the ones I wore yesterday," I grumble. "And you're avoiding my question."

He rises to his feet and stalks off. Thankfully, the boat is small and he can't get too far away from me. I chug the water, then go below deck to find him lying on his back on the bed, staring up at the ceiling. I hate the anguish in his features. Crawling onto the bed, I straddle his waist and grab his hands to thread his fingers with mine.

"Please talk to me," I beg. "You're hurting. I know it's something my dad has done, and I want to help. Maybe he doesn't know he hurt you."

He flips me hard and fast, making me cry out in surprise. Furious steely blue eyes bore into mine as he crushes me with his muscular body. "He knows, Poppy."

I blink several times, my heart racing at his sudden fury. "I'm sorry, Camden. Whatever he did, I'm sorry. I want to fix it."

"You. Can't. Fix. It."

"I'm here with you right now because you seem to think using me to torment him is a way to fix it. Don't I get a say in it at all?"

"No, Beckett, you fucking don't," he snaps. "You're a goddamn puppet in my production. Got it?"

He's pissed and trying to push me out with his hateful words. Now that I realize there is more to Camden than just being a duplicate of his dick of a father, I won't let him drive me away. For the first time in my entire life, I feel as though I'm burning from the inside out. I feel as though I'm doing what I want rather than what my dad has mapped out for me. Just knowing my dad would be pissed I'm sleeping with a Pearson, I get a thrill.

"Do you ever look back on your life and pinpoint a specific time when your life could have gone a completely different direction? Like had you just been brave for one second, you could be living your best life rather than some carefully constructed one?" I ask, changing the subject. Spending a weekend on a yacht away from my hectic life and with a man who sets me on fire, my life is beginning to unravel. It's easy to see the parts I've been doing because I have to, not because I want to. I'm unhappy. I've been that way for years.

He buries his face into my hair and inhales me, his tense body softening. Where Mateo wasn't a cuddler, Camden seems to always like to touch me in some way. Hugging me. Kissing me. Smashing me against the bed with his weight. I love it. I want to be crushed and consumed by him.

"I do," he murmurs. "I fucking do."

"Yeah?"

"There was a time with my dad..." he trails off. "I let fear cut off my tongue."

My heart aches in my chest. Eric was a terrifying

man when he wanted to be. It hurts me that Camden would have been afraid to tell his dad something important.

Running my fingers through his hair, I sigh. "I had a similar situation. With my Dad. He was pushing me toward politics like him. I wanted to teach school. He laughed and said teachers don't make shit for money. That I needed to get my head out of my ass and make my mother proud. She killed herself, and I..." a sob catches in my throat, "I wanted to make her proud."

His lips, through my hair, find my neck. "You think your mom gave three fucks about whether or not you went into politics?"

Tears well in my eyes, and I blink them away. "That's the thing. At the time, I was still so heartbroken, I listened to my dad. But truth is, Mom would have wanted me to be happy. She bought me my first globe. We'd spend hours during the summer when Dad was at work talking about where we would travel one day and what we'd see. I could name every continent and every country. Since I was a kid. I've been obsessed with geography, and still am, but it's just not a part of my life anymore."

He sits up on his elbow and brushes a strand of hair from my face. The anger is gone. Instead, he regards me like I'm a gift he's been waiting to open his entire life. I feel treasured and wanted, which is ridiculous considering I'm part of an elaborate scheme against my dad.

"You're a good politician," he says softly.

"Yeah. Because I have to be." For my dad. Because Dad insists. The bitterness creeps inside me, and for once, I don't squash it. I let it infect me. I've never told anyone how I felt before. Not even Mateo.

"You could get out." His brows furrow as he unties my top and pulls it away. "It's not too late. Go on and teach like you wanted."

My heart flutters at his words. He leans down to suck on my nipple, and then lower to my stomach. "I'm in too deep now."

He bites me hard enough that I cry out and tears form in my eyes. Then, he licks away the pain, his fierce blue eyes lifted to pin me. His hand strays south to yank at the strings on the bikini until I'm completely bared to him. I whimper when he strokes my clit in a way that he's already perfected.

"I thought you were brave, Poppy," he murmurs, then bites me again.

"I'm not, but I want to be."

"Spend some time with me. I'll teach you everything."

He works me into a frenzy, and the moment I come, shrieking out his name, he frees his dick and pounces on me. With one hard thrust, he impales me and fucks me like there is no guaranteed tomorrow. All I can do is hold on and pray we'll get a million tomorrows just like today.

THIRTEEN

CAMDEN

TWO WEEKS LATER...

FUCK. FUCK. FUCK.

I'm losing my focus. Poppy is distracting me. I spend every day when not in class in her office stealing kisses and giving her smiles—days when I should be calculating and planning. Instead of working on how I'm going to ruin them all, I help her pick out warm colors to paint the walls. I take her to lunch on the pier where we eat the best friend clams, or her apartment...where we *don't* eat at all. She teaches me important shit that will help me in my career, and then I educate her in the bedroom in the art of fucking. I'm fucking falling for her.

And I can't.

She continues to try to get me the meeting with her father, but he blows me off continuously. Of course he does. He doesn't want a meeting with Camden fucking Pearson. The meeting will go down like the rest went down with his asshole friends. But where I have blackmailed the shit out of them, I mostly want to see Marshall Beckett's face and demand to know why.

Why did he prey on me?

Fucking why?

The old familiar rage burns in my gut. Reminds me I will talk to this motherfucker and tell him how it's going to be. Poppy will hate me after. Especially when she gets drenched in the mud that will fling from her father when I smear him from one end of the country to the other. Guilt consumes me. There's no way this could not affect her—no matter how I play it. Her career is on the line because of my revenge.

But I can't stop now. I've gone nearly a decade plotting this moment. The moment when I demand answers and then gleefully go to the press with what a monster their beloved mayor is.

I've put it off long enough. Come Monday, I will march right into his office with or without a meeting, and the end will begin.

"Ooh," Poppy says as she starts packing her bag early. "We could go to that new sushi place. I've been dying for sushi. Please, Cam." She bats her lashes and grins at me. Cute as fuck.

My chest aches with emotion, but I swallow down the pain and shake my head. "Can't. I have to meet with my brothers tonight."

Disappointment mars her features. "I could come with you. I know them all. I mean, it's been years, but I think they all still like me."

I clench my jaw. "Mateo and his girlfriend will be there." It's a lie, but the nastiness feels good on my tongue. It gives me the push I need to power past her sweet smiles.

As though she's been struck, she flinches and looks away. "Oh. I'll just go visit my dad then."

The fact that she's leaving early on a Friday is admirable. She's all messy-haired bun and bright matte pink lips today. More of a vision of her older self than I've seen in the past few weeks. I love her like this. I want to throw her over my shoulder, carry her out of here, and fuck her for hours—just like I do every night since we came back from our boating weekend.

But because we've been glued together, sharing every little goddamn bit of happiness, I've forgotten my entire reason for being. I need some space to think and plot. I can't do that when my face is buried between her thighs, licking her sweet honey. My mouth waters just thinking about eating her perfect pussy out.

Focus, Camden.

"We'll go out on the boat tomorrow," I promise. "I'll pick you up at your place in the morning. Don't pack anything. I like you naked."

Her insecurities fade, and she throws herself into my arms, fusing her lips to mine. I hug her tight and kiss her hard. If I didn't think Nellie would show up, I'd lay Poppy on her desk and give her a goodbye kiss on her clit.

"Camden," she murmurs against my mouth, "I love spending time with you. I want you to know that." She pulls away and regards me with glittering blue eyes—eyes that shine with happiness and affection. "I'll miss you."

I smirk at her and playfully bite her nose. "I'll be back." I think. I hope. Fuck, I don't even know anymore.

"Promise me," she utters, her voice soft and unsure.

Images of her and I swimming in the gulf. Thoughts of her cooking with me side by side as she chatters on about how many islands there are on the planet. A picture slideshow of how perfect a boating weekend with her really is. Lots of fucking. Lots of laughing. Lots of us.

"I promise," I say finally. I mean it too.

This settles her, and she sighs in relief. "Good. I'll see you soon."

———

"I can't remember," Rowan grumbles. "I think it calls for baking soda."

"Baking powder," Lucy corrects.

"Are you sure?" Rowan attempts to read a scribbled-on recipe card.

"Flour?" Katie offers.

"No," Rowan and Lucy both bite out at once. "It already calls for flour."

I chuckle at seeing them trying to figure out Lucy's gran's famous chocolate cake recipe.

"It's baking soda," Lucy says, huffing. "I remember. It's *my* Gran," she continues, as if that makes her right.

"Remember last time you pulled the 'it's my Gran' card?" I interject from behind them. "The cake never cooked in the middle because it was too runny and we had to throw it out."

All three women turn with raised brows.

I open Rowan's cabinet and pull out a box of chocolate pudding mix. "Gran's secret was a shortcut. Remember? There is no baking soda." I shoot a smirk at Katie. "Or flour." I pull down a chocolate cake mix. "This and that. Use the directions on the cake box and add the chocolate pudding powder. That's it. This recipe card is old. There's another one in the box."

"Ohhh," Lucy grumbles. "Yeah. Ugh. How do you remember this stuff? Last time we tried to make this was like two years ago."

"For one, I'm not always getting knocked up and losing my mind to pregnancy hormones," I tease.

Rowan swats me with a dish towel. "Go away, dick. The guys are in the game room. Be quiet, though. The kids are napping. As much as Erica would love to see you, she has been a grump today."

"If you wake them, you die," Lucy threatens, looking kind of scary as she picks up a knife from the counter beside her. "Eva has decided she hates naps. Trevor finally got her down." She waves the knife in a threatening manner. "Understood?"

Katie cackles when I back away with my hands raised in surrender. Both Rowan and Lucy give her a sharp warning glare for being too loud.

"I'm out of here, psychos," I say with a grin. "Katie, run while you still can." I lift a brow. "Unless Hayden got to you too."

"Ew. Don't even start. No babies for us. Not yet."

Her happy smile tells me she hopes it'll be soon, though.

Three psychos to look forward to.

Wonderful.

I exit the kitchen and tiptoe through Rowan and Nixon's house. They bought a nice place on the beach not far from Lucy and Trevor's. It's big and reminds me a lot of our old house, but not so cold. It's warm with happiness. They're building good memories here. I'm glad too. They've both been through some shit, and Erica deserves to have the best childhood a girl could have. She may be our little sister, but Nixon plays daddy to her, and he's a damn good one at that.

After peeking in Erica's room to check on the girls, I make it down the hall to the game room. Trevor and Nixon are having a heated game of pool. Both are precise as fuck, so I can guarantee they're neck in neck. Hayden sits on the couch, his laptop in his lap, drinking a beer.

"Hey," I greet as I walk in.

Nixon nods at me as he bends over the table and takes his shot, knocking the last ball on the table into a corner pocket. Trevor curses, then grunts out a hello. Hayden glances at me and pats the sofa beside him.

"Long time, no see, asshole. I thought you died," he complains.

I laugh. "I've been busy."

"Busy fucking who?" Hayden challenges, his gaze falling to my collar. "She likes pink."

Poppy's lipstick is indeed smeared on my crisp white collar from when she attacked my neck at lunch earlier today. The memory has me smiling.

"Camden's got a girl?" Nixon asks, sauntering over to us. He sits on the coffee table and lifts a brow in question. "Since when, man?"

Trevor grabs himself a beer from the mini fridge and brings me a bottle of water before settling on the arm of the sofa. "Spill. Who's the lucky girl?"

"Poppy Beckett."

Trevor chokes on his beer. "Mateo's Poppy?"

A grit my teeth and glower at him. "They broke up. Remember?"

Nixon and Hayden exchange a shocked look.

"I've been seeing her since I started interning for her," I grumble.

"Is that the reason they broke up?" Hayden asks.

"No, asshole," I snap. "They broke up because he cheated on her with his daughter's whore best friend."

"Dude," Nixon utters. "Is everything okay? You're being kind of pissy. This was just unexpected to hear."

"I just don't want to get the third degree about who I fuck," I bite out.

"But..." Nixon's eyes flicker with questions. He wants to know why I'm fucking her. Poppy. Marshall Beckett's daughter. "Seems like a really bad idea."

"I don't really see the problem," Hayden offers. "They're not together. Poppy is hot and nice." He shrugs as if it's done in his eyes.

Trevor groans. "Except it adds more tension at the office."

Hayden laughs. "We always work our shit out, man."

"Because I love your dumb ass," Trevor says. "But

Mateo may not love your little brother anymore when he finds out he's fucking his ex-fiancée."

"It shouldn't matter," Hayden argues. "They broke up."

"Yeah, but it does matter," Trevor challenges.

Oh, fuck. Here they go again. They can't go like three minutes without fighting.

"It matters," Nixon barks out, once again eyeing me with questions. "It matters because he doesn't really like her."

I rise to my feet, and Nixon does the same.

"Not here," I snap.

"You're going to do something stupid," Nixon warns. "You've come too far to ruin your life over this."

"You don't know anything," I roar, shoving him back. "You know fucking nothing."

"I know I saved your ass that night," he bites back. "Don't tell me I know nothing. I know enough to know when you need protecting again."

"What the fuck?" Hayden demands.

I scrub my face with my palm. "Get Brock on Skype. I'm only going to say this once and I'm not going to repeat it."

"I told you not to wake—" Lucy shouts from the doorway.

Trevor walks over to her and kisses her forehead.

"Not now," he murmurs. He closes the door, shutting her out before walking back over to us. I sit back down on the sofa and let out a huff of frustration.

Be brave.

Be fucking brave.

While Hayden pulls up Skype, I think back to the time I wasn't brave. Poppy asked me if there was ever a moment I should have spoken up, and there was. I should have said something and I didn't. I was afraid. I battled the shit alone and look how far that's gotten me. Over the past couple years, my brothers and Uncle Trevor have gone through some trying bullshit. If anything, it's proven to me that they are my family and will have my back no matter what.

Just like Dad would have if he were here.

My brothers have their beef with him, but I know who he was at the center of his being.

He was protective.

————

"Where are we going, Dad?" I ask as he drives us through the city.

"Shopping," he grunts.

I'm happy to get some alone time with him, so I grin like an idiot as he drives me to the mall. We spend hours where Dad helps me pick out some suits I like and a few watches. I want to be just like my dad one day. Strong. Powerful. The toughest and richest guy around. I'm tired of being weak. I don't like being used for someone else's sick games. Eventually, we end up in an old cigar shop. I'm not allowed in here, but Dad thrusts a wad of money at the shop owner and the guy happily allows us to do whatever we want. Dad finds us two leather chairs in the corner and hands me a cigar. I don't get offered a lighter, but it's still cool. He does a bunch of stuff to prep the cigar, then leans forward with his elbows on his knees to stare at me.

"How are you doing, kid?"

His question makes me nervous, and I look over my shoulder. Marshall isn't here. I still shiver thinking he could be hiding behind the counter.

"Good," I whisper, looking down at my lap.

"Eyes here, son," he barks out. "When you're talking man to man, you look him straight in the eye. I don't care if he's bigger than you. Smarter than you. Better looking than you. Richer than you. You look at him as though you are equals, but you know deep down you are better. You make him question his worth."

I stare at my dad in awe. I've never known someone so awesome. "Yes, sir."

He smiles. "You're a good kid, and you're going places."

"I want to be like you," I tell him, beaming.

"You'll be better than me," he grunts, taking a drag of his cigar. The smoke gets blown out, billowing around us. I like the heady tobacco scent. I mimic his actions and pretend to

blow out smoke too.

"I'm doing okay," I tell him, answering his first question.

"You know if anyone hurts you, I will destroy their fucking soul, right?"

I laugh because Dad looks so fierce. If only that were true. I wish I could tell him about Marshall. Tell him about all the weird times he came into my room. All the times he'd jerk off on me and make a mess. How I got a lock on my door to keep him out. I wish I could tell him about the time Mr. Beckett really got me. The time he hurt me so bad, it hurt to go to the bathroom for days.

"Camden," Dad says. "Has anyone touched you?"

His words make me squirm. My confession sits on the tip of my tongue. Tears threaten, but I refuse to let them fall.

"I'm gross and my dad will be embarrassed of me."

"And?"

"If anyone finds out, they'll take me away from my brothers. They don't let gross boys stay with their brothers."

"And?"

"Your best friend is the boss of all the policemen. He'll put me in jail too."

"Do you believe it?"

I lift my gaze and chance a look at him. His stare is hard, and he isn't smiling at me. "Yes."

"Good boy."

"I'm doing okay, Dad," I tell him. "I'm doing okay. I may look like a kid, but I'm a man."

Dad sits back in his seat and watches me for a long time, wordlessly. Finally, he gives me a nod. "Promise me something, son."

"Yes, sir."

"If there's something I can do, you tell me. Otherwise, you do what you have to do. You're a Pearson. Pearson men are strong and don't bow to fucking anyone. Eventually, all those who wrong us, they break. They break because we break them."

I launch myself from my chair and into my dad's lap. He's stiff at first, but then he hugs me. I'll break Marshall Beckett. One day, I'll break him. I will figure out a way that doesn't make my dad embarrassed of me or get me taken away from my brothers. I'll be smart about it. I have to be.

"I love you, Daddy."

"I love you too, kid."

FOURTEEN —————

P O P P Y

AFTER CAMDEN LEFT TO GO VISIT HIS BROTHERS, I've felt brittle, and trying not to be clingy. It's hard, though. I've grown quite addicted to him. Spending every waking moment with him has been incredibly refreshing. I feel like I've crawled out of the fog that is my life and stepped into a new world. A warm world filled with laughter, salt water, and orgasms.

But this afternoon was a cold slap of reality.

He was a glimpse of the guy who stood in Mateo's kitchen that day a few weeks ago and turned my world upside down. Sure, I'd seen him around. Being engaged to Mateo, it was inevitable. But that had been the first time he'd actually entered my life and caused a stir. He made me notice him. Forced me to. And then I learned it was all for a reason.

I still don't know that reason.

Yet.

I pull into Dad's driveway and groan to see his

three best friends' cars parked out front. The last thing I want to do is see them, but I need to talk to Dad. I park my car and get out, my flip flops slapping the pavement. It feels rebellious to be wearing a summer dress rather than a suit and heels. Camden makes me brave. He urges me out of my shell.

Slipping inside the house, I walk through on a hunt for Dad. Voices carry from the living room, and before I reach the space, I listen.

"I'll figure something out," Dad snaps. "Don't I always? Just calm the fuck down."

Tension crackles in the air. I backpedal and head toward his office to wait. Like I used to do when I was a kid, I sit in his leather desk chair and spin around. But, unlike when I was a little girl, I stop and do a little snooping. I don't know his password to his computer, but do know where he hides his desk key. Once I grab it from under the keyboard, I open the locked drawers. I start thumbing through files. Most are normal financial records. But the file in the very back is labeled Project GB. I yank the folder out, only to find it empty. Dammit.

Someone clears their throat from the doorway, and I jerk to my feet. Senator John Ham glowers at me from the door. His eyes are bloodshot from drinking, and I can practically smell the booze from here.

"Oh, hey," I squeak out. "Just looking for my dad."

He stalks over to me and seizes my neck with his big hand, shocking me. "You're looking through his shit." His rage can be felt in the way he tightens his grip and cuts off my airway. I claw my fingers at his wrist to no avail.

"Ham," Dad barks from behind him. "What the fuck?"

John shakes me in his grip. "She's going through your shit! Of all times!"

"Put her down," Dad snaps at his friend.

John releases me and staggers away. Peter, the normally flirty judge, walks in scowling. Roger Bowers, the police commissioner, follows him, looking stressed. I rush over to my dad and hug him. My throat hurts, but at least he'll protect me from his drunk friends.

"What were you doing?" Dad demands.

It takes me a second to realize he's talking to me. "W-What?"

Gripping my shoulders, he pushes me at arms' length and nods to the desk. "You were going through my stuff. Why?"

"I know," I hiss. I don't really, but I want to see his reaction.

His eyes narrow. "I don't have time for your games, Poppy."

"She knows?" Peter asks. "Are you fucking kidding

me right now?"

I jerk from my dad's grip and point at him. "I know everything. I know what you did to Camden. I know it all."

The room stills for a moment, then John pulls a gun.

I scream out in horror, frozen in place.

"She doesn't know shit, asshole," he roars. "Peter, get him out of here. She's bluffing, and he's too drunk for this. Take him home and I'll clean up our mess."

Peter takes the gun from John and guides his drunk ass from the office.

"I'm not lying. How could you?" I demand, now that the room is safe from drunks with weapons. "I know all about Project GB."

Dad's face turns red, and he radiates fury. "You don't know anything about Project Good Boy, child."

"I do," I reply, my argument quickly becoming weak. Tears form in my eyes. "It's awful." Lies. I have no idea. "And I know you hurt Camden."

Dad's nostrils flare. "You're lying. Do you remember what would happen when you'd lie to me as a girl?"

I take a step back. "You'd whip me. I'm a grown ass woman, Dad. You can't whip me. What you can do is talk to me! Tell me what's going on. I want to know what Project Good Boy is and how it involves Camden."

Dad and Roger exchange hate-filled glares.

"I'm sleeping with him," I tell him boldly.

This sets him off. He charges over to me and slaps me. I'm so shocked, all I can do is hold my cheek and gape at him. The man before me isn't my father. He's angry and scary.

"Hold her hands," Dad barks at Roger as he advances on me.

"Get away from me!" I shriek, turning to try to escape. There's nowhere to go because his massive desk blocks my exit.

"When you lie, you get a spanking. When you try to manipulate your father, you get a spanking. When you sleep with a motherfucking Pearson, you get a spanking," Dad roars.

He pushes me down over the desk, and Roger wrenches my wrists behind my back, locking them in place. I scream and squirm as terror rises up inside me. I haven't been whipped since I was fourteen years old and Dad caught me making out with a boy. He bent me right over his lap, yanked down my panties, and whipped me with his belt. I'd been so horrified and embarrassed, I promised I'd never make him upset with me again.

And now, here I am, nearly thirty years old, about to get a spanking.

"Let me go!" I scream. "I'll call the cops!"

Roger laughs at this. Of course he does. The police commissioner has connections. The police won't do anything.

Dad shoves my dress up and roughly pulls my panties down my thighs. This is even more embarrassing than when I was fourteen. I hear his belt unbuckle, and then a swish as he yanks it from the loops.

"You don't know anything, Poppy," Dad snarls. "And when I'm done, you'll walk out of here and never speak a word of any of this. Do you understand me?"

Before I can answer, the leather lashes across my ass. I howl in pain and wriggle to no avail.

Slap! Slap! Slap!

A loud, ugly sob rings out in the air as he beats me.

Slap! Slap! Slap!

"I think that's enough," Roger barks out, saving me from further abuse.

Dad throws his belt to the floor and stalks off. "Get her decent and out of my house."

Roger releases me, but I'm too weak to move. I'm sobbing so hard, I feel like I might throw up. His palm caresses over my ass cheeks, and I flinch at the pain. Then his fingers brush up my thighs as he slides my panties back into place.

"Your father loves you," Roger says softly. His finger boldly touches my pussy between my legs over my panties. "We all do. Just be a good girl and let us look after you."

He then drags my dress back down over my ass and helps me stand. My knees buckle, and he pulls me to his chest. I cling to his shirt for fear of hitting the floor. Tears stream down my face and drip from my jaw, soaking us both.

"Calm down, Poppy," he coos. "He is looking out for you. Trust me. If he didn't, he'd have let John have his way. Who the hell knows what John would have done? He's always had a thing for you, but he looked like he wanted to kill you." He kisses my head. "You're safe as long as you just stop trying to pry into your father's business."

He pulls away slightly and grips my chin, tilting my face up. I try to move my head, but he's stronger. His lips press to mine, and I manage to push him away.

"Don't touch me," I hiss through my tears. "Don't fucking touch me."

He rushes me, no longer trying to play the nice guy, and pushes me against the wall. His meaty hand gropes my breast as he glowers at me. "None of this happened. You walk out that door and pretend none of it happened. Then you can continue fucking that piece of shit if you want. You can go on to become lieutenant governor. Your whole life continues as planned. Do you understand me?"

"Fuck you," I hiss.

He grinds his laughable erection against my thigh. "If I have to in order to make you understand how goddamn serious I am, I will. You are fair game now. Tread carefully."

I freeze in his grip. "Please let me go."

"Tell me what I need to hear."

"I know nothing," I whisper. "I saw nothing. I heard nothing."

He tries to kiss me again, and I go limp in his grip. Finally, he releases me. "Good girl."

FIFTEEN

CAMDEN

"WHAT'S GOING ON?" BROCK DEMANDS THE moment his face shows up on the Skype screen.

Ethan and their girlfriend Camila pop in behind him, worried looks on their faces.

"Pearson business," Hayden snaps, shooing off the other two with a flick of his wrist.

Nobody corrects Hayden and says Trevor isn't a Pearson, and that's fine by me. Trevor was always like a brother to my dad. He can stay for what I'm about to say. If anything, it makes me feel closer to my dad.

"I'll meet you guys down at the beach later," he tells them both. When they're gone, he turns to regard us with a frown. "What's going on?"

"Camden has to tell you all something," Nixon says.

I let out a huff of resignation. "When I was a kid, around the time Mom left, Marshall Beckett abused me."

"Almost," Nixon corrects. "He fucking tried, but we took care of it."

"He what?" Hayden growls.

"It's why it's a bad idea for him to fuck Marshall Beckett's daughter," Nixon explains.

"You're fucking Poppy?" Brock asks, clueless until now. "She's hot."

"Back up to the part where you said her fucking dad hurt you," Hayden snarls.

"Almost—" Nixon starts again.

"Shut up," I hiss, fury blazing through me. "Just shut the fuck up."

Nixon, my best friend and protective older brother, gapes at me as though I've killed his dog, until he starts clicking the pieces into place. "No."

I grit my teeth. "Yes. Nixon walked in on Marshall doing some sick shit and scared him away."

"I tried to tell Mom," Nixon chokes out. "She..."

We all know what happened after that. She ran off anyway. Ran off and ended up dead, buried in our neighbor's yard.

"I'm going to kill him," Hayden growls.

"You and me both," Trevor hisses.

Brock mutters, "Fuck," over and over again.

I straighten my back. "He was a sick fuck. He came back." My eyes bore into Nixon's. "He came back plenty.

And then, one time, he made me want to die."

Hayden rises from the sofa and starts pacing. "I will destroy him." His rage matches that of our father. I love Hayden. Seeing him like Dad all those years ago makes me love him even more. Hayden has been here for me acting as a father figure since Dad died, and I appreciate that more than he will ever know.

"Who fucking does that to a kid?" Brock demands. "What kind of sick fuck does that?"

Trevor trembles with fury, his teeth grinding to dust as he barely keeps from exploding.

"An asshole who is going to die," Nixon says coldly. "He will fucking die for this."

I reach over and clutch Nixon's shoulder. "You're married, man. You have Rowan and Erica and a baby on the way. Don't go getting stupid on me."

"Rowan's pregnant?" Brock asks.

"Maybe show up more than twice a year and you can keep up with the family," Hayden snarls.

I stand and walk over to Hayden to grip his shoulders. "Calm down."

"Me?" Hayden roars. "Me calm down? How the hell can I calm down knowing what happened to you? I'm going to ruin him!"

I turn and look them each in the eye. "Marshall Beckett is why I've wanted to go into politics since everyone can remember. Dad said if someone hurts a Pearson, you break them. I've spent my entire life working on a plan to break him."

"Eric knew?" Trevor demands.

"No," I tell him. "He knew something happened, but I didn't tell him. Marshall had me scared. He took advantage of a scared little boy and I believed his threats. But now...now I know better. I know I hold all the cards."

"Poppy," Nixon breathes. "You're going to...what? Fuck with her just to fuck with him?"

It's more complicated than that.

"It started as that, yes. I wanted to use her to get me meetings with Marshall and his fuckface friends. I wanted to get in and let them know I have shit on them."

"What kind of shit?" Trevor probes.

"The kind of shit that gets grown men thrown in prison for life." My friend Cronk dug up enough dirt on them to bury them forever.

"What are we waiting for? Why toy with Poppy?" Hayden asks. "Why aren't we taking this shit to the police and making him pay?"

"Because I want to see the look on his face when I tell him he's fucked. I want to look him square in the eyes and make him feel like a piece of shit. I want to tell him I've defiled his daughter like he defiled me. I want to destroy him. Smear him. Run his name across every tabloid before sending him off to prison." My chest heaves with fury. "I want to ask him why."

Nixon scowls. "Because he's a sick fuck, that's why."

"I just need to see what sort of bullshit excuse he gives me," I utter softly. "I just need to hear it."

"He won't apologize," Nixon warns.

"I don't want an apology," I snap. "You can't say sorry and make that shit go away. I don't want it to go away. It's built the man I am today. I want him to see that. To realize he created the very beast that will tear his proverbial throat out. I just need that meeting. Then I'll send what Cronk dug up to the FBI and let them do the rest."

"It'll ruin Poppy too," Nixon tells me. "You know that."

I hate that my brother always reads me better than anyone else. He knows I like her. What started out as a revenge plan has evolved into me actually fucking liking her.

"So I'll ruin her." I shoot him a hard glare. "It was always the plan."

"Sometimes plans change," he mutters.

"You do realize," Trevor says slowly, "when the media gets a hold of this, it'll expose all the bad stuff that happened to you. The reporters will pick and pick and pick at that wound. Are you ready for that?"

"A true leader shows what kind of man he is by how he handles the bad situations. I'm fully prepared to face this head on. I've thought about this for a long time. The actual events that happened feel like a bad dream. But making him pay is a reality. I want it more than my next breath. I'll take whatever the media throws at me. Then I'll move on with my life and make my way to the fucking White House where I belong."

"Well, okay then," Trevor huffs. "Tell us what we can do to help."

"We get him that motherfucking meeting," Nixon growls. He turns to me and pierces me with an intense look of fierce love and protectiveness—the same look he gives our little sister and his wife, Rowan. "I will get you that meeting, brother."

———

Poppy: Lady Vindicta.

Her text was sent late last night, and I squint against the morning sun to reread it. I was supposed to pick her up from her apartment.

Me: On my way.

"I'm going to be a big sister," Erica tells me proudly as she stabs at her pancakes. She doesn't quite understand her family dynamics yet, and no one corrects her. Hell, it's almost too complicated for us to understand, much less explain to a young girl.

"I heard, little bit." I walk over to her and kiss the top of her head. "When are your parents going to bring you on the boat? I got you a pink Minnie Mouse fishing pole."

She squeals and starts begging Rowan to take her today.

"Today I have plans, but maybe next weekend," I tell her.

"Next weekend works better," Rowan says. "Remember, Aunt Lucy and Aunt Katie are taking us shopping today."

"I want to go fishing," Erica pouts.

"I thought you wanted to go to the Disney store." Rowan raises a brow at her.

Poor kid looks positively torn. I save her from her misery.

"If you go shopping with Mommy today and go fishing next weekend, then you get to do both. You don't have to choose." I wink at her, and she grins. "See you ladies next week."

I feel lighter during the drive to the marina. Getting that load off my chest to my brothers and Trevor was oddly a relief. I knew tempers and emotions would flare, but we got through it. We're Pearsons, after all. We get through everything—as long as we do it together.

I park and make it out to where my yacht sits. When I step inside, there's a trail of Poppy's mess and it warms me. I like her mess all over my things. She's still in bed when I get below deck, so I undress completely and slide beneath the covers beside her. I brush her hair away from her sleeping face and stare at her.

I'm going to make a mess of our lives.

As soon as I get that meeting with her dad, all hell will break loose. She'll be forced to choose. And my girl isn't brave. She won't choose me. She'll choose him. He's her dad. Not to mention, I'll be the reason her political career will be destroyed.

Guilt, an unfamiliar emotion, plagues me.

I don't care.

This was always the plan.

Her eyes flutter open, and the striking blue glimmers at seeing me. It makes my heart thunder in my chest.

I do care.

Fuck.

"Hey," I rumble.

She leans forward and kisses my lips. "Hey."

"Miss me?"

When she doesn't respond, I pull away to look at her. Her features crumble before my eyes as an ugly sob makes her entire body tremble.

"Baby," I murmur. "What's wrong?"

She clings to my chest and presses her face to my flesh. Her tears soak my skin as she cries. I stroke her hair, my nerves threatening to give me an anxiety attack.

When her sobs die down, I push her onto her back again. She winces as though she's physically in pain. I rain kisses down all over her face. I'm not sure what the fuck is wrong with her, but I've never seen her so broken. It unnerves me.

"Tell me what to fix," I murmur.

"I'm sorry."

I cock my head to the side and study her features. Her cheeks are red and tearstained. Her nostrils flare with each ragged breath she takes. She's so beautiful. Hurting and broken, yet so striking.

"Why are you sorry?"

"Because he hurt you."

I clench my jaw. "Poppy," I warn.

"He hurt me too."

At this, I startle. "What?"

"Did...did my dad molest you?" Her bottom lip trembles.

I give her a clipped nod even though she doesn't deserve the answer. It's risky. She's technically Team Beckett, not Team Pearson.

"You want to meet with him to confront him?" she

asks.

"Yes."

"And then what?"

"Destroy him."

She winces, but doesn't move away from me. Her eyes are sad as she looks me over as if to memorize my face. "I can't stop you."

"It'll destroy you too," I warn.

"Then you can put me back together."

Her words give me hope that maybe I don't have to choose. Maybe I can still get my revenge and get the girl. Would it be so fucking bad to take her as my trophy? I could shield her from whatever the press dishes out. She'd fit right in with Lucy and Katie and Rowan. The very idea of her one day at their side with her own pregnancy hormones fighting over a chocolate cake recipe has me filling with this need to possess her. To stamp my mark on her soul and make her mine. I've been utterly obsessed with her from the moment I was introduced to her all those years ago when she was way out of my league. When I thought Tampa's Golden Girl would always be an image I whacked off to—never the real thing.

Yet here she is.

Spreading her legs and inviting me inside her.

Kissing the hell out of me like her life depends on

it.

She loves me too. On some unspoken level, she feels the same intense way I feel about her. Mateo treated her like an arm piece. A shiny trophy to cart around. But she's more than that to me. She always has been. For nearly a decade, she's been the center of my revenge plan. The silver lining. The prize at the end. I knew eventually I'd fuck her and then ruin her dad. I didn't ever count on fucking and falling for her. Certainly didn't plan for her to fall right down the hole with me.

My mouth consumes hers as I thrust into her wet heat. I fuck her sweetly like we do sometimes and kiss her reverently. She's mine, and no matter what happens with all this, she'll still be mine.

Even if that means changing the plans.

Destroying him means destroying her.

And I don't think I can do it.

Fuck.

Love changes everything.

———

I chose her.

Chose her over my plan to destroy *him*.

Some days, I can't believe it. Me. Camden fucking Pearson. The man who has planned and planned for so damn long, threw everything away for a woman. I'm thinking with my heart and not my brain. It's almost inconceivable. When my brain takes over and the anger surges through me, I wonder if I've made a mistake—if I've been duped.

But all it takes is her honest, loving smile first thing in the morning to remind me I chose well. Poppy may have been pretending in every aspect of her life, but not with me. With me, she gives me her real self. The fun, bubbly, happy-go-lucky girl who used to be my babysitter. And when she sees the storm brewing in my eyes, she comforts me with her touch, her body, and her words.

She's fucking healing me.

It's been weeks since I admitted what her father did to me. Weeks since she told me what he also did to her. The waters had been rocky, but we found balance together. Just having someone to talk to—someone who understands me and wants to help me—has been incredible.

I want to cling to my past and use it for an accelerant on my hate, but she forces me to let go. She's a distraction. A gorgeous one at that. For years and years, I've let this revenge plan drive every action in my life. My past has paved the way for my future. It's exhausting to continuously be making moves for an ultimate agenda.

She lets me rest.

I'm safe with her. To just close my eyes and live in the moment. I don't have to think ahead or dwell in the past. I just enjoy her scent and her soft skin. I live for the sounds she makes right before she comes. Breathy and beautiful.

I'd thought Poppy was a tool to use for me to destroy others.

Turns out, she's a tool to heal.

I should have known someone as sweet and perfect as her couldn't be used for dark deeds. Poppy is light and laughter and love.

She's mine.

"New Zealand?" she asks as she sips on a blue coconut and rum fruity drink she loves so much at our favorite clam restaurant.

I shake away my daze and take in her sexy appearance today. Under the bright Tampa sun, she's this city's golden girl. No fucking doubt about it. Her blonde hair is still wet from her shower earlier where I took her roughly and passionately from behind. A pair of my sunglasses she stole from me sit perched on top of her head, revealing her pretty blue eyes to me. Her face is bare, not a speck of makeup. The freckles on her nose peek back at me, and I smile. She looks gorgeous as hell.

"You want to go to New Zealand?" I smirk at her.

"Who doesn't?" She grins and takes another sip of her drink. Those things get her wasted fast so I'll have to make sure she doesn't drink too many. Stress continues to be her captor and the perpetrator of her still-constant headaches, but she seems happier. Despite the fact that she knows her father was my abuser and has written him out of her life, she's finding joy again.

"We'll go to New Zealand then, baby," I tell her as I reach for a cheesy roll. "That's more than a weekend trip, though. Where do you want to get away for a couple days, Miss Globe Trotter?" I munch on my roll while I wait for my answer.

Her nose scrunches as she looks off behind me toward the bay. It's something she does when she's thinking. I'm still every bit in tune with her tells, but no longer to use them against her. Now, I study her so I can draw more smiles from her. So I can hear her laugh or talk rapidly about something she's excited about.

While she thinks, I drag my gaze down her outfit. A bright yellow sundress that shows off all her lovely curves. It didn't seem that long ago that she was here with me wearing a suit and sadness. All that pretending was wearing her down. Today, she's a poster child for freedom. Sure, she has to be at the office tomorrow, but this afternoon, she's happy and free.

"We could go to LA and visit your brother," she muses aloud.

"I've already walked in on one too many threesomes," I say with a snort. "Pass."

She giggles. "I like Brock, but I don't want to see his ass."

"My ass is better," I say, flashing her a wicked grin.

"I don't doubt that for a second." She sips her blue drink again. I love how her pink lips have turned purple from the drink. Later, I'll suck that bluish-purple tongue until I turn it pink again.

"LA is scratched. Where else?" I have a break coming up at school and would like to go someplace with my girl.

My girl.

Sounds fucking awesome.

"What about New York?"

"You want to meet Grandad?" I ask, grinning.

"I mean, he sounds like a great guy. You think he'd buy me a Bugatti too?" she teases. "I want pink. Like Lucy."

"Lucy has a Maserati." I try not to cringe at that awful pink car.

"Depending on how much Grandad likes me, I may ask for both." She's just fucking with me, but she's cute as hell doing it.

"Grandad will love you," I assure her. "He's a Pearson after all."

She reaches across the table and takes my hand. We thread our fingers together. This is right and perfect.

I chose wisely. With my heart. Love is a much more palatable emotion than hate. So sweet. The bitterness that usually clings to me is nothing but a fading aftertaste. Love is a flavor I'll certainly get used to, and soon.

"Let's visit your Grandad," she says firmly. "I'm sure he misses you and would love to hear how well you're doing in life."

"College is damn near kicking my ass because my girlfriend demands all my time to go on vacations," I tell her playfully. "You call that doing well in life?"

She rolls her eyes. "You're the only person I know who aces all their exams and assignments without cracking a book. I studied my ass off in college and barely made it out of there with passing grades. You're kicking college's ass, not the other way around."

When she starts to pull away, I tighten my grip on her fingers. "Poppy..."

Her brows pull together in that concerned, protective way she gets over me if she thinks I'm mentally struggling. I hate that she feels responsible for what her father did. It's not her fault. "What is it?"

I grit my teeth together and look up at the sky. Clear and flawless. The present is easy and free. Because of her. I let out a sigh, ridding myself of the negative energy that sometimes brews to unhealthy levels inside me. She helps me purge it all. "Thank you." I look back at her, pinning her with an intense stare.

"For what? I didn't do anything."

I pull her hand closer to me and kiss the inside of her wrist. "Thank you for being you. For choosing me."

Releasing my hand, she stands and walks around the table to sit in my lap. Her arms wrap around me in one of her comforting hugs. I squeeze her middle, kissing her collarbone.

"I'll always choose you," she whispers.

I tilt my head up and stare at the beautiful woman. Mine. "Promise?"

"Always." Her lips press to mine and she kisses me in a way that feels as though she's sealing a vow. The little cracks in my heart are filled each time I'm with her. "You're mine, naughty Camden Pearson. Don't go forgetting that."

I stare at my angel, shining brightly under the sun. All for me. A reward for an awful life endured. "I'll never forget, baby."

I kiss her so deeply, so intensely, she'll never forget she's mine too.

At one time, I thought revenge was the answer, but my revenge would destroy the one I love—and fuck, I do love her. So revenge has been deleted from the plan. The plan now resembles that of my brother Hayden's. Love. Marriage. Babies. I want whatever I can get with Poppy

Beckett. Revenge would steal my only bit of happiness, and I'll be damned if I let that be stolen from me. The past already took so much. It fucking owes me this.

It's a hard pill to swallow, giving it all up for her, but at the end of the day, I choke it down and drink from her. My sweet, beautiful Poppy. She's the only medicine I need.

"Camden," she murmurs against my lips. "I lov—"

I devour her sweet sentiments with a crushing kiss.

I know, Poppy, because I love you too.

SIXTEEN

P O P P Y

TWO MONTHS LATER...

I WALK OUT OF THE OFFICE ON THE FIFTY-SEVENTH floor and head toward the elevator bank. My heart is in my throat, but I feel good. This was the right thing to do. Two months ago, when my boyfriend admitted my father had molested him, I revealed to him everything that had happened at my dad's house. John Ham pulling the gun. Roger Bowers holding me down as my father brutally whipped me. The way Roger groped and tried to kiss me. It shamed me to tell him, but I owed him those facts. Relationships are built on trust. Camden needed to know I was on his side.

It took some time to cool him off. He wanted to beat them to death, but I finally calmed him down. It was then I mentioned to him that I thought maybe they were doing other things that were bad. Like Project Good Boy. As soon as I mentioned the name, Camden exploded. He revealed everything his friend Cronk had discovered on their computers.

Hundreds and hundreds.

So many children.

Camden wasn't the only one.

I'd thrown up that day and cried until I was tearless. Camden, strong as hell that man, held me through it all. My father is a monster. End of story. His friends are monsters too. Camden had been working tirelessly all these years to obtain evidence against them all—to see how far the evil roots were. Because it was a judge, police commissioner, senator, and mayor, he was tight lipped and careful. Bided his time. He was ready to go to the FBI with it all, but then this thing between us exploded.

The Camden who walked into Mateo's that night months ago is not the same one I'm madly in love with now. The Camden I know and adore would do anything to protect me. Even from the onslaught of the media. Because the moment he goes forward, my career will be over.

But it's not about me.

It's about him and those other children.

His stubborn ass refused to give me what I needed. The proof. He said to just move on. I can't move on. I know, and knowing means I have to proceed. With or without him. So, today, I decided to go forward and tell my story to the *Tampa Times*. Everything I know. Everything Camden has told me. It'll be enough to push him to hand over the evidence to the FBI and bring that ring of sick fucks down—especially my father.

It hurts because he's my dad.

But my dad has been gone for some time. He morphed into this monster after my mom died. A monster I don't recognize. When he chose his friends over me and whipped me, I knew there was no getting him to step up and be a man about this. My dad is shady and sick. There is only one way out for him—prison.

Once the *Tampa Times* releases the story, Camden won't hold back anymore. The only reason he's held off is to protect me. To keep me from getting shamed along with my father. I'm a big girl, though. Tampa's Golden Girl may be tarnished, yet again, but she's with the future president of the United States. If anyone can dust her off and pick her up again, it's him.

My phone buzzes, and I smile upon seeing a text from Camden.

Cam: Where are you?

I text out a reply.

Me: On my way.

I'm nervous about having dinner at his brother Nixon's. I've gone over there a few times and really like his wife, Rowan. She's an adorable pregnant woman, and her daughter, Erica, is a spitfire. They're the cutest family ever and it gives me hope that maybe Cam and I can have something just as special.

What I'm nervous about is Mateo being there. Everyone will be there. I haven't seen Mateo since that night. He knows I'm dating Camden. Hayden, Cam's oldest brother, proudly blasted that fact out over dinner one night. But knowing and seeing are two different things.

I drive along the road toward Nixon's admiring the view. Camden and I spend a lot of time on his boat. He's having a house built near his brother, and I've been told that's where I'll live when it's finished. I love it when he goes caveman on me.

Cars already line their driveway by the time I arrive, and another bout of nerves threatens to consume me. Camden will be pissed that I've gone around him and forced his hand. But then, like the beast he is, he'll run forward to do damage control on our end. He'll make my father pay. And Camden will come out great on the other side. His future is solid. His future with me is impenetrable.

I'm barely out of the car when he emerges from the house. He looks good in a black polo and cargo shorts. At ease and happy. Shit. What have I done?

I panic as I close the door and worry I've made the

worst decision on the planet. His smile falls as he stalks over to me. I'm drawn into his muscular arms and let out a sigh when he squeezes me.

"What's wrong?" he demands.

I tilt my head up and frown. "I did it."

He blinks at me. "Did what?"

Desperately, I kiss his mouth, because it's better than saying the words. He's stiff at first, but then his palms are roaming my ass and squeezing. His teeth nip at my lip before he pulls away.

"What did you do?"

"The right thing," I mutter.

His face transforms from worried to briefly angry. Then, he smiles. Beautiful and heartbreaking. God, I love him.

"Which newspaper?" he asks, knowing me better than I know myself.

"*Tampa Times.*"

He kisses my nose. "Good choice, baby. They're honest and will make a big fucking stink over this. As it should be."

"You're not mad?"

He laughs. "You chose me over that filthy bastard. Of course I'm not mad. It means you love me."

I hug him and sigh. "More than anything."

"I won't let anything happen to you," he vows. "If

you want to—"

Shaking my head, I look back up at him. "I'm done. I want out. Maybe take some time off to travel or just relax. I don't know. And maybe I can teach once the dust settles. This is the life he chose for me, and I don't want it. I just want you."

He pulls away and reaches into his pocket. "I got you a present."

I gasp at the sparkly watch. "A Cartier Tank Anglaise!" His love affair with watches is catching. I've become quite obsessed with each one he's now given me. "It's beautiful."

"Just like you," he says sweetly, winking at me. He can be so charming when he wants to be. I let him put the watch on me and then we hold hands. "Ready to go meet that fucker?"

I groan. "Shouldn't we be more worried about how they'll respond once they realize I've sent your story to the press? Are your brothers going to kill me?"

He squeezes my hand and tugs me along behind him toward the house. "Nobody is going to kill you. They've been begging me to move forward with this. You did everyone a favor."

"I did it for you," I tell him. "And for them."

We both grow serious. The nameless children. Just faces in a catalogue. Disgusting horrors. All of that will be ripped apart and exposed. Cronk says they're just pictures and there isn't any proof of any illegal sex trafficking or anything, but we'll leave the FBI to uncover the truth. What I do know is they're all guilty of having that sick shit on their computers and my father is guilty of molesting Camden when he was a boy. Hopefully, this will end now. Those four bastards won't go through life as though they're untouchable. They are all going down.

Camden guides me inside to the flurry of activity. People are laughing and drinking. Kids are shrieking. The house smells like barbeque. I love it. It's chaos and happiness. Uncontrolled and wonderful.

"What do you want to drink?" Camden asks, kissing my forehead.

"I'll have what you're having." I wink at him.

Water. We're having water.

My guy abides by the rules and keeps his reputation squeaky clean. And drinking underage is a risk to his future. A presidential hopeful can never be too careful. He saunters off to grab something to drink, and I find the girls.

"Isn't she the cutest?" Lucy chirps when I walk over to them. She's squeezing Brock's girlfriend's cheeks and gushing over her.

"Adorable," I say, laughing. "Where are the boys?"

Camila grins. "Trying to teach Erica how to surf.

Brock is great at surfing, but not a good teacher. Lucky for him, Ethan is. They're figuring it out. How have you been?"

We chatter and catch up. I want to keep this moment frozen in time. Where everyone is happy. I don't want to tell them by the time they go home tonight, one of the Pearsons they know and love will be the center of every tabloid from here to California. Camden is confident we'll be fine, and I trust him.

He sidles up behind me and offers me a bottle of water. I lean my back against his chest and sigh.

"I love you," he murmurs against my ear. "You were always mine. I was always coming for you. He may have had you for a bit, but it wasn't ever going to stop me."

I follow where he gestures to Mateo across the room. Mateo has his son on his hip and is grinning widely. His girlfriend is fussing over the boy's collar. Their family dynamic seems natural and right. Nothing about Mateo right now is stiff and mundane. We were a pretend, wannabe family. We could have never been that. I wouldn't want that because I have this. Turning, I stand on my toes and kiss Camden.

"I love you too. Thank you for coming for me," I say, smiling.

His grin is devilish as he stares at my lips. "And you'll be coming for me tonight. You know *Lady Vindicta* loves to hear you scream."

———

"Is it bad?" I ask, groaning from where my face is buried under the pillow.

"I imagine the shit is hitting the fan right about now."

I tug off the pillow and smile at him. "But..."

"But we're miles from land with no cell service. They can interview us when we get back," Camden says as he walks through the cabin, his swim trunks low on his hips. His smile is wicked when he notices me checking out his defined muscles in the perfect shape of a V.

"How long have you been up?"

"Right along with the sun. It's near noon, baby. Time to get up."

So cheerful considering his life is getting cut open as we speak. Somewhere away from here, the news is blowing up. We'll get hit eventually, but for now, we're safe.

He plants a kiss on my forehead before disappearing into the kitchen. I shower and dress before joining him for breakfast. It's funny to watch him with his brothers' women. They like to fuss and baby him. He just soaks it up and pretends he doesn't even know how to use the microwave. Then, when it's just us, he cooks and is far from the baby they see him as. I like that he shows a different side to me. A side that doesn't always smile. A side that broods and gets lost in his anger. The real side. And because of this, I show him the real me. The me who doesn't want to be a lawyer or get into politics. The me who would rather live with her toes in the sand and her nose in a book. The one who would rather spin a globe with children and dream of places we'll one day travel rather than go toe-to-toe with suits in a courtroom.

Camden frees me.

After breakfast, he stops the boat and dives in. I watch him swim for a while before joining him. He always looks like a predator in the sea, swimming like a shark. And I willingly offer myself up to him every time—his victim ready to be bitten.

I hold my nose and jump off the side. The water is cold today—too cold to be swimming—but I know we won't stay out long. Just as I start treading water and bob at the surface, he attacks. His strong arms wrap around me and he hauls me over to the ladder. Once I'm secured and safe from sinking, his lips attack mine. He yanks off my bottoms, and for a moment, I fear I've lost yet another pretty swimsuit in the ocean. But then he tosses them into the boat as I wrap my legs around his waist.

"Poppy," he growls as the crown of his cock pokes at my opening.

I wriggle and attempt to slide down his shaft, but

his strong hand at my hip stops me. "What?" I whine.

He chuckles, his hips barely flexing, teasing me even more. "I love you."

"And I will love you if you just fuck me already."

A laugh erupts from him as he throws his head back. I admire the way the water runs down his neck corded with delicious muscle. Even his Adam's apple is hot. I want to lick it. I love everything about him. Even when he teases me. When his amused eyes meet mine again, they glimmer with desire. Fire and fury. A look he reserves only for me right before he devours me.

"You already love me," he says smugly, inching his way into me.

I dig my heels into his ass and use all my strength to bring him all the way in. Once he's seated deep inside me, I let out a breath of relief. "I love you more now."

He palms my breast roughly and bites my jaw. His hot breath tickling me has my pussy clenching around him. "You'll love me even more in just a few minutes."

With those words, Camden fucks me hard enough against the ladder, I'll be sporting bruises for days. His palm abandons my breast to finger my clit. A few expert strokes and then he's sending me into oblivion.

Intense pleasure explodes within me, obliterating everything but him.

He's right.

I love him even more.

And that love just keeps on growing.

EPILOGUE ——————

C A M D E N

EIGHT MONTHS LATER...

"**B**ABE," NIXON SAYS AS HE WALKS OVER TO Rowan, who's nursing their son, "we're going to go fishing."

"Fishing, huh?" Poppy asks, tilting her head up to look at me.

"I want to go fishing!" Erica yells, making her baby brother jump.

"Not today, baby doll," Nixon tells her. "Camden and I have to talk man to man."

I flash Poppy a pleading look. If Nixon needs me, we don't need little prying ears. Luckily, my girl is understanding.

"We don't need silly boys to plan our own fishing expedition," Poppy tells her. "Let's go look at your globe and figure out where we'll go without them."

Erica bounces on her feet and tugs Poppy from

the couch. Before she gets too far away, I grab her left hand and bring it to me so I can kiss it. She's wearing her newest Michele Deco Diamond bracelet watch I got for her on Valentine's Day, but that's not what I want to see. What I want to see is how obnoxious the diamond on her ring finger looks on her tiny hand. I love that it's ridiculous and over-the-top expensive. I thought she'd give me grief for it, but diamonds really are a girl's best friend. She loves that ring. She loves what it signifies more. Next fall, we're going to get married. This beautiful, brilliant, funny woman will be mine in every sense of the word. The Beckett name will be banished, and another Pearson will enter the fray.

"You're beautiful," I mouth to her.

"You're mine," she mouths back.

I'm grinning as I follow Nixon out the back of the house to his new boat he has docked. It's a speedboat and not nearly as badass as *Lady Vindicta*, but *Psycho Queen* makes up where she lacks in looks and luxury in speed. She's a monster that eats distance like it's her fucking job.

We board the boat and Nixon wastes no time firing up her engine and blasting us along the coast. We're miles away when I finally yell over the noise.

"Where are we really going?"

His jaw is set and the muscles in his arms are taut as he navigates the waters. "We have a meeting."

I lift my brows. "Anyone ever tell you you have the whole Dexter Morgan vibe going on now that you're a boat man like me?"

He grins and tips his head. "I'll take that as a compliment."

"You would, asshole."

We both smile as he drives us to our location. My brother has always had my back. Like now, he's doing this for me. It was always in our plan. Sure enough, he pulls up to the dock behind Poppy's childhood home. Where Marshall fucking Beckett still lives. That part really does my head in. He tattled to the FBI about his friends' illegal activities that were more far reaching than even I had realized in exchange for immunity. I'd been pissed as fuck, and Poppy cried. The bastard may have lost his job, but he still lives his life out in early retirement while his friends rot in jail.

Nixon pulls up beside the dock and jumps out. He ties the boat quickly and motions to a cabinet. "Put that on and hand me one. We can't risk it."

I pull out the ski masks and gloves, shooting him an amused stare. "Why does it entertain me to know you have this shit ready?"

He shrugs. "Because you're a happy bastard, I guess. Fuck if I know. Cover your face and your prints. Our meeting may get ugly."

It can't get too ugly, though. He knows I need my record clear and free for my future. And he sure as fuck won't jeopardize his happiness with his family. Too much is at stake.

We're just going to talk.

That's all I ever wanted.

After we don our disguises, we prowl up the back of his property and sneak up to the back door. Nixon starts pulling tools out of his pocket to pick the lock. I pull on the sliding glass door and it opens. He snorts and puts the unneeded tools away. We slip inside and creep through the house. It stinks. Like old fucking man and stale liquor. He's just about bankrupted himself over attorney fees according to Cronk who likes to hack into his bank accounts and keep me apprised on shit. I can't wait until this bastard loses everything.

We find him sitting at his desk looking haggard and old. He's fallen asleep in his chair, wearing just his boxers. His hair has turned white over the past months, probably from stress. He's pathetic.

And yet...

I'm that little boy terrified as fuck.

My feet come to a stop, and I can't move forward. Nixon squeezes my shoulder. "I've got you, man." He pushes past me and slams a fist on the desk.

Marshall jolts awake and stares up at him in horror.

"Who the fuck are you?"

Nixon pulls a gnarly looking knife from his belt as Marshall scrambles for his desk drawer. I rush over, finding my courage, and yank the drawer open. A gun. I jerk it away before he can get his hands on it. Realizing he's stuck, he raises both palms.

"I don't want any trouble, boys," he says.

Spineless bastard.

"We're not boys," Nixon growls. "We're your worst fucking nightmare."

"I don't understand," Marshall mutters.

"We're here for the meeting you owe me," I bite out.

His eyes widen in horror. "Pearson? You sound just like your fucking dad."

"And thank fuck your little girl is nothing like you," I snap back. "Did you find out I'm going to marry her?"

"She's a bitch like her mother. I should have done her like I did Lana," he bellows, his face turning purple with fury.

Nixon and I exchange a look.

"What did you do?" Nixon demands.

"You're going to kill me anyway," Marshall grumbles. "I think it would be good for you to destroy Poppy by telling her her mom didn't kill herself. She stumbled upon some shit I had on my computer and threatened to move far away with *my* daughter. To turn *me* in. So I dragged that bitch into the bathroom and helped her cut her wrists open. Stupid cunt." He points at me. "Go tell your fiancée I would have done the same to her had I been smarter."

"Pick up that pen," I bellow. "I want you to write a motherfucking apology to your daughter. For being a sick pig who hurts children and preys on the weak. Do it and make it believable." We all know he's not really sorry, but Poppy deserves an apology. She deserves to know the truth. "Tell her how her mother was forced to kill herself."

"And if I don't?" he taunts. "You'll kill me anyway."

"My brother will do no such thing," Nixon growls. "Because he's innocent and pure. I, on the other fucking hand, will peel your skin off square by square and feed it to you until you write the goddamn letter."

The pussy of a man jerks his hand to pick up the pen. Nixon walks up behind him to read over his shoulder. He nods when Marshall sets the pen down.

"Now what?" Marshall demands.

"I want to know why," I croak out.

He pins me with hate-filled eyes. My first inclination is to look at the floor, but Dad's words are forefront in my mind.

"Eyes here, son," Dad barks out. "When you're talking

man to man, you look him straight in the eye. I don't care if he's bigger than you. Smarter than you. Better looking than you. Richer than you. You look at him as though you are equals, but you know deep down you are better. You make him question his worth."

I glower down at Marshall like he's the scum of the earth. He is. About time someone calls him on it.

"I don't know why," Marshall snaps. "There. Happy? Are you going to kill me or what? I'm over this shit."

Again, Dad is in my head, walking me through this every step of the way.

"Do what you have to do. You're a Pearson. Pearson men are strong and don't bow to fucking anyone."

"Now," I say as I hand the man the gun, "you're going to do what you should have done a long time ago. Now, you give back to the motherfucking community, Mayor."

He eyes the gun like he might try something funny, but Nixon thumps him in the back of the head, reminding him he could slit his throat before he even managed to point the gun at either of us.

"If you're waiting for an apology, it's not fucking coming," Marshall snarls.

"It was never about an apology," I tell him coldly. "It was about revenge. It was about seeing you break, motherfucker. It was about getting the last laugh."

"Eventually, all those who wrong us, they break. They break because we break them."

Dad's words are on repeat as I make a motion with my fingers in the shape of a gun and push it into my mouth.

"Bang," Nixon growls from behind him.

The old man startles and stares at the gun. "At least tell her I love her."

"I'll do no such thing," I tell him, shrugging. "I'm too busy telling her how much *I* love her. How she'll soon be a Pearson and won't have that fucking last name attached to her. Don't worry, I'm taking care of her in all the ways you failed, old man. Time's up. Bang."

He raises the gun to his mouth, and Nixon steps aside.

Pop. Splatter. Thunk.

Nixon laughs, and I let out a sigh of relief. My brother's mask is covered in brain matter and his green eyes gleam wickedly. But he's innocent. Every bit as innocent as I am.

"Hands are clean, Mr. President," he tells me as he walks around the desk and grips my shoulder. "Let's go home to our girls."

I turn, and he stops me.

"I'm sorry," he says, all humor gone from his eyes.

I hug my brother. "I didn't come here for an apology." Pulling apart, I lean my forehead on his. "I came to break him like he tried to break me."

He smiles. "When are these assholes ever going to learn?"

"And what lesson is that, big bro?"

"We are motherfucking Pearsons. And Pearsons are unbreakable."

I follow him out to his boat, and we slip away. It isn't until we've dumped our ruined clothes miles out in the ocean—Dexter Morgan style—and are speeding back home that we speak again.

"I think Dad would be proud how we turned out," I tell him.

"That prick would never admit it," he groans.

I smile as I look out at the beautiful waters. I can almost smell the cigar from the shop that day. Hear the deep timbre of Dad's voice. Feel the love radiating from him despite him hardly ever saying it.

"I love you, Daddy."

"I love you too, kid."

"He'd be proud," I tell him confidently. "He'd be proud we broke him."

"And that a Pearson is going to rule the world one day," my brother says, laughing.

"Not the world. Just the country."

"Close enough," he says. "Now, don't fuck up. Keep your head on straight. Marry the girl. And go take what's yours."

I grin at him. "It was always the plan, brother. Always the plan."

ENJOYED THIS BOOK?
MEET THE OTHER SONS

Four Sons Series by bestselling authors

J.D. Hollyfield, Dani René,

K Webster, and Ker Dukey

Four genres.

Four bestselling authors.

Four different stories.

Four weeks.

One intense, sexy,

thrilling ride from beginning to end!

This series should be read in order to understand the plot.

A FOUR SONS STORY

Who's the daddy now?

NIXON

KER DUKEY

NIXON

BY KER DUKEY

I am devious, a dark soul, and son to a dead man
—or am I?
I plan many moves ahead to get the result I want.
Her.

Things may be complicated, but we were always destined for
each other.
I'll protect her from any threat and defend my interests, even
if it means going against my own brothers.

My name is Nixon Pearson.

I'm ruthless and deadly, but also devoted.
People may think I'm young and naïve,
but that's just a mask I wear to fool them.

This series should be read in order to understand the plot.

A FOUR SONS STORY

There's a new
sheriff in town…

HAYDEN

J.D. HOLLYFIELD

OTHER BOOKS IN THE
FOUR SONS SERIES

HAYDEN

BY JD HOLLYFIELD

I am a hothead, a wild card, and son to a murdered man.
I crave the things I can't have and don't want the things
I can.

Now, I'm left to pick up the pieces—stitch our family
back together with a damaged thread.
This isn't the life I envisioned. And to make matters
worse, the women in our lives are testing the strength of
our brotherhood.

My name is Hayden Pearson.

I am the eldest—a protective, but vindictive son.
People may think I'm too young to fill our father's shoes,
but it won't stop me from proving them all wrong.

This series should be read in order to understand the plot.

A FOUR SONS STORY

Why choose one when
you can have both?

BROCK

DANI RENÉ

OTHER BOOKS IN THE
FOUR SONS SERIES

BROCK
BY DANI RENÉ

I am strong, athletic, and son to a man I always wanted to be. I had made plans, thought I was on that path, and then a bullet stopped not just my father's heart, but mine too.

I've been living a life I'm not meant to.
I want more. I want to escape.
And I found someone who's given me a love I never thought possible.

My name is Brock Pearson.

I am a free spirit who found happiness in an unexpected place. People assume I'll be another heir to our empire, but my heart belongs elsewhere.

This series should be read in order to understand the plot.

BOOKS BY K WEBSTER

The Breaking the Rules Series:
Broken (Book 1)
Wrong (Book 2)
Scarred (Book 3)
Mistake (Book 4)
Crushed (Book 5 – a novella)

The Vegas Aces Series:
Rock Country (Book 1)
Rock Heart (Book 2)
Rock Bottom (Book 3)

The Becoming Her Series:
Becoming Lady Thomas (Book 1)
Becoming Countess Dumont (Book 2)
Becoming Mrs. Benedict (Book 3)

War & Peace Series:

This is War, Baby (Book 1) - BANNED (only sold on K Webster's website)
This is Love, Baby (Book 2)
This Isn't Over, Baby (Book 3)
This Isn't You, Baby (Book 4)
This is Me, Baby (Book 5)
This Isn't Fair, Baby (Book 6)
This is the End, Baby (Book 7 – a novella)

2 Lovers Series:
Text 2 Lovers (Book 1)
Hate 2 Lovers (Book 2)
Thieves 2 Lovers (Book 3)

Alpha & Omega Duet:
Alpha & Omega (Book 1)
Omega & Love (Book 2)

Pretty Little Dolls Series:
Pretty Stolen Dolls (Book 1)
Pretty Lost Dolls (Book 2)
Pretty New Doll (Book 3)
Pretty Broken Dolls (Book 4)

The V Games Series:
Vlad (Book 1)

Ven (Book 2)

Taboo Treats:
Bad Bad Bad – BANNED (only sold on K Webster's website)
Coach Long
Easton
Crybaby
Lawn Boys
Malfeasance
Renner's Rules

Carina Press Books:
Ex-Rated Attraction
Mr. Blakely

Four Fathers Books:
Pearson

Four Sons Books:
Camden

Standalone Novels:
Apartment 2B
Love and Law
Moth to a Flame

Erased

The Road Back to Us

Surviving Harley

Give Me Yesterday

Running Free

Dirty Ugly Toy

Zeke's Eden

Sweet Jayne

Untimely You

Mad Sea

Whispers and the Roars

Schooled by a Senior

B-Sides and Rarities

Blue Hill Blood by Elizabeth Gray

Notice

The Wild – BANNED (only sold on K Webster's website)

The Day She Cried

My Torin

El Malo

Sunshine and the Stalker

Sundays are for Hangovers

Hale (only sold on K Webster's website)

ACKNOWLEDGMENTS

Thank you to my husband. You're my awesome hero. I love you so much!

A giant thank you to Ker Dukey, J.D. Hollyfield, and Dani René for taking the Four Fathers and Four Sons journey with me! So much fun, ladies!

A huge thank you to my Krazy for K Webster's Books reader group. You all are insanely supportive and I can't thank you enough.

A gigantic thank you to those who always help me out. Elizabeth Clinton, Ella Stewart, Misty Walker, Holly Sparks, Jillian Ruize, and Gina Behrends—you ladies are my rock!

A big thank you to my author friends who have given me your friendship and your support. You have no idea how much that means to me.

Thank you to all of my blogger friends both big and small that go above and beyond to always share my stuff. You all rock! #AllBlogsMatter

Monica with Word Nerd Editing, thank you SO much for editing this book. You're a rock star and I can't thank you enough! Love you!

Dani, thanks for formatting this book!

A big thanks to my PR gal, Nicole Blanchard. You are fabulous at what you do and keep me on track!

Lastly but certainly not least of all, thank you to all of the wonderful readers out there who are willing to hear my story and enjoy my characters like I do. It means the world to me!

ABOUT K WEBSTER

K Webster is the *USA Today* bestselling author of over sixty romance books in many different genres including contemporary romance, historical romance, paranormal romance, dark romance, romantic suspense, taboo romance, and erotic romance. When not spending time with her hilarious and handsome husband and two adorable children, she's active on social media connecting with her readers.

Her other passions besides writing include reading and graphic design. K can always be found in front of her computer chasing her next idea and taking action. She looks forward to the day when she will see one of her titles on the big screen.

Join K Webster's <u>newsletter</u> to receive a couple of updates a month on new releases and exclusive content. To join, all you need to do is go <u>here</u>.

STALK LINKS

Facebook
https://www.facebook.com/authorkwebster

Blog
http://authorkwebster.wordpress.com/

Twitter
https://twitter.com/KristiWebster

Email
kristi@authorkwebster.com

Goodreads
https://www.goodreads.com/user/show/10439773-k-webster

Instagram
http://instagram.com/kristiwebster